For Marissa

Your continued support means everything to me. May I be your pillar as much as you are mine.

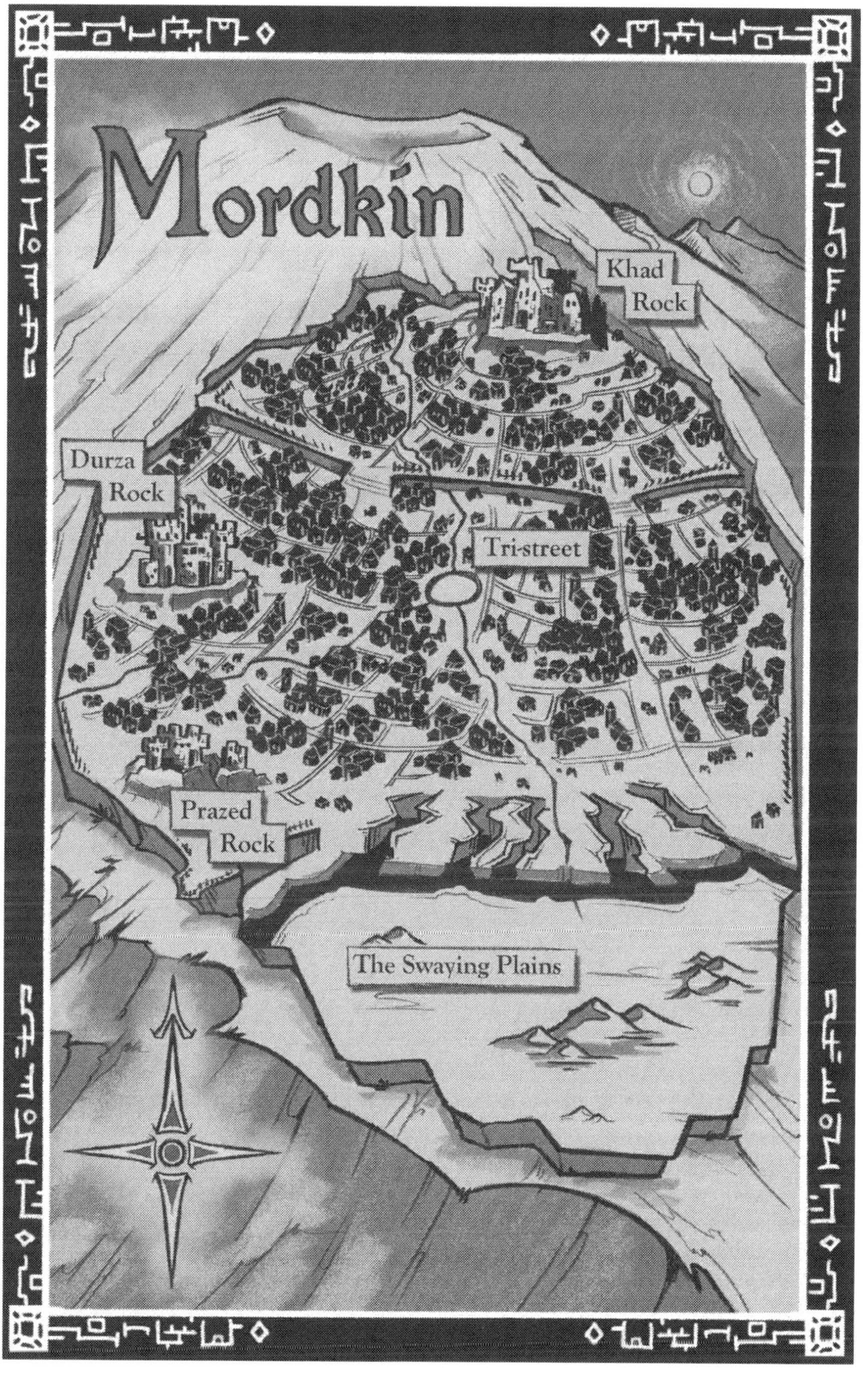
Mordkin
Khad Rock
Durza Rock
Tri-street
Prazed Rock
The Swaying Plains

Author's Note

A piece of advice I often hear as a writer is to try your hand at writing in every genre, and in 2024, I set out to do just that. I bought *The Anatomy of Genre* by John Truby, a book that identified and broke down 14 major genres to their plot beats, themes, and special quirks, and started at the top with the goal of writing a short story in each of these genres.

And that's where King Maker began.

It was my short story for the "gangster" genre, modeled after Truby's outline and exemplified by the movie I have heard so much about, yet have never seen: *The Godfather*.

However, I didn't think a purely gangster tale would captivate me enough to devote an entire month to writing. So, I decided to combine the genre with fantasy—one of my favorites to write in. Inspired by Tolkien's Erebor and Moria, the dwarven kingdoms carved into the very mountains of Middle Earth, I felt I had a strong story idea to begin writing. Certainly strong enough to captivate me while going through the (planned) three revisions.

I did not, however, account for how disastrous that first draft would be. Trying to fit so much of Truby's outline—one meant primarily for screenwriters, not authors—into a short story of about 25 pages proved to be more of a challenge than I had anticipated, and after one month, I was left with a piece of writing that was incredibly flawed, and that I dreaded coming back to.

But I'm stubborn.

Before King Maker, I had shelved 2 projects in a row: my second (unpublished) novel, and my action genre short story that was part of this same "genre marathon" project of mine. I did not want to shelve a third.

Luckily, I didn't *hate* the story. I recognized that what I had was a story I enjoyed that would either need a lot of building up and improving (far more than my planned "one month"), or a lot of cutting down and diminishing.

So I made my decision, and now, after nine drafts and more than triple its original length, *King Maker* is finally finished, and I can italicize the title. Yay!

Except.

There's so much left on the cutting room floor when it comes to writing—or any creative endeavor, really. To put it into perspective, the final draft of *King Maker* is around 29,000 words. However, over the course of eight months and nine separate drafts, the total number of words I wrote for this story was over 150,000. When reading *King Maker*, you are literally only reading a *fifth* of what was put into the story. That's dialogue changes, added and removed scenes and characters, new plot beats, and so much more that are, traditionally, gone. Lost. Left alone to never see the light of the printed page and die in obscurity, only having ever lived inside the author's head, and on their hard drive, and perhaps rightly so.

But perhaps not.

Growing up, I loved watching movie special features. In the era of physical media and DVDs that I grew up with, watching deleted scenes, director's commentaries, and behind-the-scenes documentaries were a part of the experience for me. I mean, I grew up in a family that didn't even fast forward through the commercials before reaching the main title scene/film because those were *part* of it (and now those trailers serve as a time capsule that is always interesting to see).

Today, with mostly digital media, that passion for film and video games lives on through content creators, documentarians, essayists, and others who have taken those features to video sharing platforms and social media.

But for books, special features don't...really exist. They might for grand epics in the form of appendices, maps, spell lists, family lineages; but for small stories like *King Maker*? Not really. Or, at least, not often.

Which is why I've chosen to include my own special feature at the back of this book.

Now, I could choose to include each of *King Maker*'s nine drafts here, causing the book to balloon to the length of a full novel with only a fifth of the story, but that feels wrong. As a reader, I would feel cheated. It would cease to be a special feature in my eyes, and instead become some authorial ego boost under the guise of "not letting a single word go to waste." But I also can't imagine not sharing at least some of *King Maker*'s journey with you.

So, I've decided to split the difference.

The first part (and vast majority) of this book is *King Maker*. Complete, refined, and ready for readership.

The second part, however, is King Maker: the first draft. Unedited. Messy. The same story, only very, very different. Hopefully, in lieu of showing you every little word that went into the final story, this first draft can give you a bit of the "behind the scenes" feeling I want to offer.

Regardless of how you choose to read, I hope you enjoy *King Maker*. Where it ended, and where it began.

Thank you for reading.

With a Smile,
Quain Holtey

Acknowledgements

There are so many different voices that contribute to a final, published book. Now, with any luck, I won't forget any of them, but I also have a terrible memory. So, if you were a part of the creation of *King Maker*, and I don't credit you here, you have full permission to yell at me.

First, my wonderful support system: Marissa Holtey. You helped and encouraged *King Maker* before you even knew I was writing it, and you continued to help in every possible way after I sat you down and forced you to read it through that first time. You're my first beta reader, my idea bouncer-offer, and my number one fan; and you always have been. Thank you.

To my beta readers. In no particular order: Marissa Holtey, Paige Holtey, Karen Bowden, Katie Jensen, Nick O'Donnell, and Charles Painter. Your feedback, big or small, pushed *King Maker* to being better than I could have made it alone. I am in awe to have such amazing people in my life willing to read and critique my work. Thank you.

To Robin LeeAnn, thank you for being my incredible editor. This is my first published work that has been professionally edited, and working with you was such a breeze. You made *King Maker* read so much better than I ever could have managed alone. I may have gotten it 85% of the way there, but your edits lifted it up to 100%. Thank you.

To my amazing cover and interior map artist, Kathleen Harwood. You brought Riddin and Mordkin to life in a way I could only dream of. You took my rough ideas, terrible reference photos, and nitpicking feedback and created something incredible that I (and many others) am proud to put on my shelf. Thank you.

To Isaac Nelson, Aezik's namesake, and without whom *King Maker*'s audiobook would have never happened. You're on your way to greatness, and I'm so happy to be along for the ride. Thank you.

To you. Yeah, it might be cliche to acknowledge the reader, but I don't care. However you're reading this, it means you've taken a chance on me as an author. You support me. Thank you. Hopefully one day we'll meet (if we haven't already) and I can thank you in person. Bring *King Maker*, I'll be happy to sign it!

Finally (in case that last one didn't catch everyone), to all of the wonderful people who were a part of *King Maker*'s journey who I haven't named. Thank you. I swear I'm not ungrateful, I just have a terrible memory.

Now, without further ado, let's begin our story.

If I remember correctly, it all starts in a bar...

King Maker

RIDDIN SIGHED AGAINST the chronic pain in his hip as he pushed the small pouch of wooden coins toward the barkeeper. Again. "Come on, Yaro. Take it. Use it to repair the bar, aye?"

Yaro ignored him, instead choosing to stare intently at the debris at his feet while he swept. It wasn't surprising. The barkeeper's willful ignorance was why Riddin came to this bar in the first place; it was preferable to the outright contempt he received from others. But still, it was disappointing. After three whole years, the dwarf still refused to meet Riddin's eyes.

Knowing that wouldn't change now, Riddin placed the pouch on a table that was still upright and then left through the gaping hole that was now the bar's storefront.

Cold rain dripped from the stalactites that clung to the city's ceiling. The towering homes and storefronts had been carved from the very rock that had supplied them with the precious metals and gems that adorned every facet. Lamps and torchlights danced against the brilliant wet surfaces. Beautiful reflections only interrupted by the crowd of snarling, cursing dwarves who jeered insults at one another from across family borders.

The rain made Riddin's muscles tense as it struck his bald head. His tailored clothes—the swirling red and black pattern of the Khad family, accented by garnet and silver inlays—tightened across his narrow shoulders. The chill sent a dull ache through his hip at the point where it met his metal prosthetic. For someone as accustomed to torment as he was, it was almost painful. Almost.

But it had been a dry season, and rain meant clean streets and filled aquifers. So, when he had finally walked over the broken stones and shattered glass to stand next to Aezik and the two stubborn dwarves writhing in pain on the ground at their feet, he was smiling.

Aezik couldn't have been more different from Riddin. Aside from his own baldness—shaved to match Riddin's natural alopecia—Aezik was a colossus of a dwarf. He stood head and shoulders above everyone else in Mordkin, and still another pair of shoulders taller than Riddin. His sleeveless arms showcased bulging muscles as they hung carelessly over the leather-wrapped shaft of the war hammer that was draped across his broad shoulders. As Riddin approached, Aezik's thick beard hid the grin that crinkled his eyes.

"I appreciate your help, Aezik." The hydraulics in Riddin's prosthetic bent his knee as he knelt beside one of the writhing dwarves on the ground. "Next time, try not to launch them through a window?"

Aezik brushed off the request with a shrug.

Riddin studied the supine dwarf—now that he wasn't threatening Riddin in his favorite bar. He was Unnamed, judging by the state of his clothing. Rough-forged armor chafed his thick dwarven skin that wasn't covered by scraps of cloth.

Riddin glanced up. Across one of the street's borders, he noted the finely crafted metal disiplate of the Prazed family. Which meant this Unnamed must have been a Prazed before he had been stripped—his armor now nothing more than a cheap mimicry of what he used to wear.

Except for a splash of color in the cloth band around the Unnamed's arm.

Fresh cloth. Cloth that had needed to be woven and bleached before it had been dyed green with copper. Quite a lot of work for a dwarf otherwise wrapped in cheap rough steel. The same work reflected on the armbands of the three *other* Unnamed who had come into the bar with him and who had fled slantward in the violence.

"Interesting." Riddin held an open palm out above the dwarf's mouth.

The dwarf was still breathing, despite the crater in his chest from Aezik's war hammer. And if he could breathe, he could talk.

Riddin looked up at Aezik. "Good of you not to kill him.

Though in the future, you could make it less of a spectacle. Still, at least now I can ask him some questions."

"*Questions.*"

It was the other dwarf on the ground who had spoken. A short-bearded dwarf with sharp eyes and sharper eyebrows. Viz.

"Fuck its questions!" Viz shouted. He struggled to his feet, a limp in his step where Aezik's war hammer had struck. "I say we kill the Unnamed bastard. Like true Khad!"

Viz wasn't speaking to Riddin, or even to Aezik. He spoke to the other dwarves spread throughout Tri-street, whose screaming threats of violence across family borders had been temporarily quelled by the real violence that had exploded in front of them. Dwarves whose rage gnawed at Mordkin's peace and turned the ice-melt rain into rising steam.

Aezik shifted the war hammer across his shoulders, sliding his hands down the helve. The leather-wrapped handle crackled with his tightening grip.

Viz paused at the threat, his own one-handed half hammer only partly drawn from his belt. The other dwarves behind Viz matched his unease.

Riddin placed a thin hand on Aezik's arm, and the giant froze—poised and still. He offered Viz his best smile, one he had practiced so many times for exactly this kind of situation. Still, practice was not the same as confidence, and his other hand fell to rest on the handle of the strange weapon at his hip.

"Easy, Viz," he said. "I just want to find out why not one,

but four Unnamed ventured into Yaro's Bar tonight. And why this one"—he tapped his prosthetic foot against the Unnamed with a hollow metallic thud—"went through all that trouble just to insult me."

"Because you deserve it," Viz said. "Just like I deserve to see the Unnamed's blood stain the street! Who gives a shit about what it does or why it does it? And why should we give a shit about what a damn *krevtish* has to say about—"

Aezik's arm disappeared from beneath Riddin's hand as he brought his war hammer down. It struck Viz's shoulder, breaking it with a crack like quarried stone. The stubborn dwarf collapsed back onto the ground with a scream that earned cheers from the Durza and Prazed dwarves watching from their borderlines.

From the surrounding Khad, however, it earned resentment and fury. Hands went to their weapons. Bodies lowered in readied crouches. Aezik brought his war hammer back up, adding to the tension in the air.

But a fight wouldn't break out. Not if Riddin could help it.

Riddin drew the strange weapon from its sheath at his hip. He didn't point it at the Khad—he wouldn't dare—but an unknown weapon in the hands of an intelligent dwarf was enough to swallow the fury on the street.

It was exactly what Riddin had hoped for. Why he had named his gun Peacekeeper.

"Take Viz back to the Rock," Riddin said to the surrounding Khad. "Have someone see to his injuries."

The Khad stayed where they were, and he suppressed a sigh. He hoped Peacekeeper would have been enough, but the moment of authority he felt was now replaced by the truth. The Khad were looking at the gun in Riddin's hand, but none of them were looking at *him*.

In the pause, Aezik moved his war hammer, pointing the broad stone head at Viz on the ground, then up the city's incline—hillward, toward the Rock.

Riddin wanted to think he had a part in the dwarves' sudden jerk to action. That they had listened to his words belatedly. Or that the threat of Peacekeeper had given the necessary pause for Aezik's orders to find purchase, but he knew the truth.

Aezik was the strong one. He was a threat, and that earned him respect. Even if the other dwarves couldn't understand the giant's loyalty to Riddin—couldn't understand why he had stayed by Riddin's side after their years of working together at the aquifers—they understood Aezik's strength.

In contrast, Riddin wasn't even worth looking at. So, despite being thankful for Aezik and knowing the giant dwarf's loyalty, Riddin's envy stoked the small flame of resentment back to life in his chest.

He watched as the last of the threatening dwarves scrambled into an alley with Viz on their shoulder before sheathing Peacekeeper again. He dropped his head back with a sigh and stared up at the city's ceiling, letting the rain sprinkle his face. He took in a deep breath and searched, as he so often did, for peace amid the stars in the stone.

Set into the stalactites, deposits of cloudy quartz—long-since deemed too worthless to mine in a city filled with riches—twinkled with the reflected light of the city below. Eternal and unmoving. He had thought they were cold and indifferent when he was younger, but now, in a city on the edge of violence, he found comfort in them. Hope. Down here, on Mordkin's streets, the divide between dwarves was ever-present: carved into the very ground by the borders between families, but up there? Up there, it didn't matter where the city lights came from: Khad, Durza, or Prazed. Up there, there weren't three families.

There was just one Mordkin.

Riddin brought his thoughts down from the stars and back to Tri-street—jeering dwarves all around him, a dying dwarf at his feet, and a giant at his side. His anger and resentment taken by the stars—his jealous flame extinguished—and he found his clarity once again.

"I'm sorry, Aezik," Riddin said. "I saw how they listened to you, and for a moment there, I...I hated you. Envied you." He looked at the giant and chuckled. "How ridiculous is that?"

With no anger of his own, Aezik lifted his war hammer and draped it over his shoulders once again. His arms hung loose over the helve. A rare smile with too-few teeth split his thick beard as his body shook with his silent laughter.

"Thank you. And thank you for helping with Viz. He might be family—as much as he likes to pretend otherwise—but he deserved it. And now that that's all settled"—Riddin returned his attention to the Unnamed at his feet—"how about we meet our new friend?"

The Unnamed had stopped writhing in pain and was now lying still on his back, eyes closed and breathing ragged. His hand absently scratched at the edges of the indent in his chest.

Riddin's knee creaked on its metal hinge as he knelt and placed a heavy hand on the wound. Gray dwarven eyes laced with pain shot open to meet his gaze.

"At first, I thought you had stepped into Yaro's Bar by mistake," Riddin said.

The dwarf's eyes fluttered as he flirted with unconsciousness. Riddin lifted his hand from the dwarf's chest, watching as air returned unimpeded—well, almost unimpeded—to his lungs.

"Then you singled me out." His fingers brushed the dwarf's green armband. "You and your Unnamed friends."

The dwarf's hand smacked Riddin's to the side and grabbed a hold of the armband himself. "Not...Unnamed." His defiant words ground against his broken ribs, but they were dry and strong.

Aezik's blow hadn't punctured his lungs then.

"Tharkar..."

"Tharkar?" The name stirred distant memories, ones of childhood stories and adventures told to Riddin before he could read. They sparked an urgency in him that he hadn't expected. A hope. "Did Anez send you?"

"*King* Anezendir," the dwarf barked with pride. He opened his mouth again, and Riddin leaned in closer to hear what he had to say.

And the Tharkar spat in Riddin's face.

Aezik sloughed the war hammer off his shoulders, but Riddin held up a halting hand. Riddin couldn't let the giant crush the Tharkar's head in. Not now. Besides, there wouldn't be anyone left under the mountain if Aezik killed every dwarf who spat on him.

That said, the Tharkar *had* insulted him. Again.

Riddin redrew Peacekeeper from his hip and rested its barrel against the Tharkar's broken chest. Pushing through his own discomfort, he pressed the gun into the cratered metal—into the Tharkar's broken ribs and crowded lungs. The flimsy armor bent and cracked beneath the pressure, and the dwarf's breathing became quick gasps as pain brought the dwarf back into consciousness. He focused on Riddin with seething eyes filled with long-smoldering hatred.

"Let's try that again," Riddin said. "What does *King* Anez want? Why did you come here—you and your friends?"

"Wants to...meet you," the dwarf said.

"Why?"

The dwarf's eyes lulled, and his head dropped back to the ground. It might have been due to the pain, but it felt an awful lot like spite against Riddin, and that was something he didn't have time for.

He grabbed the Tharkar's chin and shook his head back and forth. "Tell me why!"

Aezik jostled Riddin from behind, the force of it nearly knocking him over. He turned and stared up at the giant—a shout on the edge of his lips—but found Aezik's gaze locked onto something in the distance. Further down the street—hillward, where Viz and the others had gone—came an unmasked fury framed in coarse black hair with daggers already drawn and flickering with blue lightning.

Vira.

Which meant Riddin was out of time.

He pivoted back to the Tharkar and, with teeth grinding against the disdain of the act, pressed Peacekeeper into his chest again. Hard. The dwarf would have screamed under the pain if he'd had any air in his lungs—but his rage-filled eyes were alert once again, wild and directionless.

Riddin grabbed the dwarf's chin with his other hand and focused that rage on him. "Where?" He released Peacekeeper's pressure a bit. Just enough to let air wheeze back into the dwarf's lungs. "Meet. Anez. Where?"

"The...lake."

The lake.

"I understand." He twisted Peacekeeper, releasing the pressure while angling the gun's barrel up toward the dwarf's heart.

Perhaps if Vira weren't descending upon them, the Tharkar could have lived. Now though? His death was inevitable. The least Riddin could offer was some mercy.

"For what it's worth, I'm sorry."

He squeezed the trigger.

There should have been a click. A sharp, metallic click as the gun's trigger mechanism struck the spin wheel, which should have agitated the gun's elektrum core. And there should have been a half second whirring sound as the elektrum's energy wound through the frequency coil and condensed into a bullet of pure lightning that would have shot through the Tharkar's chest, obliterating his heart and ending his pain.

Instead, there was silence.

Riddin pulled the trigger again. Still nothing.

Again. Nothing.

He didn't get a fourth attempt.

Vira's boot struck his head, and the world split into sparks of white. He flew off the Tharkar and slid across the rain-slicked ground.

Riddin had found there was a freedom that came with pain. Pushed to an extreme, it consumed everything. Every thought. Every emotion. Every sensation. If it was bad enough, it could even make him forget the pain in the first place. He had discovered this freedom through beatings, abandonment, and neglect. Through experience.

Vira had discovered it through affliction.

She knew exactly how hard to strike him to inflict pain without granting him any of the peace offered by its extreme. Torture was her talent, and because of that talent, Riddin maintained his awareness as he came to rest on the ground, as Aezik knelt to protect him, and as he looked back to where the Tharkar still lay.

Blood spilled from the parallel arc-burned slashes on the Tharkar's throat. His wheezing vanished beneath the gurgling sound of drowning, and instead of the swift death Riddin had tried to grant him, the dwarf's last fight for his life was reduced to a pathetic, writhing misery that lasted almost an entire minute.

It felt like an eternity.

Riddin forced himself to watch, feeling as though his acknowledgment was the least the Tharkar deserved in his final moments. Vira watched too. Her ferocious smile stared the Tharkar down while she pinned his struggling arms to his sides until the last of his life seeped out, and red mixed with the drizzling rain beneath the mountain.

And then Vira and her wrath were upon Riddin.

She pinned Riddin to the ground, her two daggers pressed against his throat. The refined elektrum gems, fitted into the pommels, sent electricity coursing down the blades. The electricity arced and burned lines against his bare skin. His muscles seized, and his heart quickened.

Close behind, Aezik brought his war hammer over his head—clearly intended to bring it down on Vira's back—but Riddin held up a halting hand. Killing Vira wouldn't solve anything.

Riddin fought through the seizing electricity to open his mouth and speak. She spat on him. Then, as though the first time wasn't enough, she collected her saliva and spat on him again.

So, Riddin chose to wait.

"Fucking useless," she said. "You can't kill a fucking Unnamed even when it begs you? Here. Let me show you how."

With a flick of her hand, she nicked his neck with one of her daggers. Electricity jolted into his wound, making his skin itch and burn. It traveled down to his gut. His lungs seize. His body convulsed.

The cruel smile returned to Vira's lips. "What's the matter? Nothing to say? Come on. Show me how *strong* you are, *krevtish*."

Like the Tharkar before him, he took in quick, shallow breaths as he built up enough air to speak through clenched teeth. "Man Speak...doesn't belong...on dwarven tongues. Sister."

Her smile turned into a snarl as she forced a short rush of air through her nose—half disgust, half amusement. She stared at him with an unfocused gaze as if she was staring through him and into the ground, somehow meeting and avoiding his eyes at the same time. Then she leaned in close, pressing her daggers against his skin and sending pain throughout his body.

"Deformed, weak, and spineless." Her rage whispered. "What would you know about being a dwarf? What makes you so special? Why was something like you chosen over me?"

Riddin could feel blood escaping through the thin cut on his throat. He could see himself dying, pathetic and writhing on Tri-street while every dwarf in the city watched.

The klaxons blared. Low at first, they slowly built to a clamoring roar from every direction that clashed at Tri-street.. Flinching, Vira brought a hand up to cover one of her ears from the sirens. Sirens that only blared once a year, but every dwarf knew what to do. The watching dwarves meandered away, called by the city alarms to either return to their Rocks or clear the streets.

Vira returned her not-quite gaze to Riddin with a scowl. "Always a lucky little *krevtish*, weren't you?" she asked, her voice barely audible through the noise. Then her snarl flicked with a smile that betrayed a cruel idea. "Father may not let me kill you, but I can still remind you of your place. Consider this a gift, *brother*."

With a final stroke, she stabbed one of her daggers into Riddin's prosthetic knee. The elektrum-heated blade easily slid into the metal, and electricity seized its mechanics. It writhed out of his control like a snake, and the insulating leather barrier where the metal met his hip burned.

She jumped off him, dodging Aezik's swinging war hammer as it chased her through the air. She landed, poised and ready to strike with a challenging smile, as Aezik stood guard over Riddin.

Free of the elektrum's power, Riddin took in large gasping breaths that eased the burning in his lungs. His heart raced, and his body ached with the effort of seized muscles finally allowed to relax. The electrified air tasted of metallic plasma as he choked it down. By the time he caught his breath, and the acute pain was replaced by the familiar ache of the chronic, Tri-street was already abandoned—save for him and Aezik.

Vira was nowhere to be seen.

Aezik stood by Riddin as Riddin struggled against his broken prosthetic and rose to his feet. The hydraulics inside it had ruptured, and it refused to bend at the knee or ankle, making it no more than a straight, heavy piece of ornately cast metal.

Riddin looked down at the only other dwarf who remained on Tri-street, the corpse of the Tharkar Vira had killed. The one he had *tried* to kill.

"Peacekeeper didn't work," he said. Through the wailing sirens, it was to himself more than anything. He drew the gun and aimed it down at the dead dwarf's body before pulling the trigger again. For good measure.

Still nothing.

"No click." He sheathed the gun. "Not even a misfire. Something's wrong with the internal mechanism again. I'll need

Orin's help with that." He looked down at his broken prosthetic. "And this."

He lifted his gaze to the center of Tri-street—the city's center. There, the carved grooves that separated Mordkin into its three uneven parts met at a large bronze plate carved with the portraits of their respective sides' family monarchs.

King Roan Khad's portrait was strong. Powerful. His posture was straight, the crown on his head square and perfect. The bronze robbed the portrait of any color, but his clothes still held the swirling, smoke-like pattern of Khad as though the carver had stitched the metal itself.

Soon, the monarchs of each family would stand on the bronze and talk. An annual conclave set in the open streets as a sign of power, even as the klaxon alarms called for those streets to be cleared for the monarchs' protection. For their privacy. No one knew what the monarchs discussed on the bronze. Prolonged peace, trade negotiations, sustainability...

One day, Riddin would stand on the bronze with them. One day, he would finally bring the families of Mordkin together. For now though, he could only hope that when the three names under the mountain met, and Roan Khad stood tall and imposing on the bronze, Riddin's father looked as strong as his portrait.

Except...for the first time in two hundred years, there was a fourth name in Mordkin. One that was uniting the Unnamed. One that called Anezendir their king.

The Tharkar.

"Come on, Aezik!" Riddin yelled over the sirens. He twisted his uncooperative leg and brushed the giant's arm as he trundled past. "We'll pay Orin a visit soon enough. First, I need to speak with my father."

* * *

THE CONSTANT BREEZE, carried from the ventilation shafts along the city's edges, that swept through Mordkin's slanted streets pushed against Riddin's back as he and Aezik climbed hillward. Frost crawled across his rain-soaked clothes, and the city's warmth was replaced by a coldness that matched its abandoned streets. Elektrum-powered lamps glowed orange with a false promise of warmth, gleaming off the reflected gems and metals of the city.

The cold tightened Riddin's broken prosthetic. It bit his left hip while his right burned with the burden of his stumbling gait. He tripped often, and though he never fell, he felt like a child bumbling around on feet he wasn't used to.

Aezik, of course, never mentioned his fumbling. Aezik was the only person in the city who had never harassed him for his deformity. When they had first met, he thought it was because of the giant's muteness, but over time, he realized—or at least chose to believe—that even if Aezik could speak, he would never insult him. He had earned Aezik's loyalty working in the aquifer, somewhere between designing tools to ease both of their burdens and sharing his vision of the future for Mordkin.

A future that, because of Anezendir, might be closer than he thought.

As they walked, Riddin cast his gaze down side alleys and hidden crevices cut into the streets. Though they were cleared of Khad, he had expected to find Unnamed stragglers, even this high up the city's slant, yet there were none. Not fewer than normal or less than he expected. But *none.* Though the sirens had called for the streets to be cleared, there had always been some Unnamed who remained without homes or Rock to return to. Where were they now? Perhaps they all had fled slantward with the sirens, but he doubted that.

Maybe, instead, they all wore the green armbands of the Tharkar. Perhaps they all called Anezendir their king, and they did have a Rock to return to. Or a lake.

At the top of Mordkin's slant stood Khad Rock. Its towering peaks merged with the mountain's starry canopy, and its turrets and walls dripped like ornate, melting wax from the ceiling. Above it, bolstered by the Rock's single imposing form, bulged the underside of the city's aquifer. The city's roads spread from Khad Rock like it was the center of a spiderweb.

Riddin climbed the front steps up to the stone doors that towered three stories high. Siege weapons—ballistae, crossbows, and spears—trailed his approach from the surrounding balconies above. Weapons that would have been left derelict and crumbling in the two-century-long peace between families if not for the dwarves ordered to train with and maintain them. The soldiers didn't shoot Riddin, but the fact they trailed someone who wore Khad colors so diligently betrayed their desire to.

It wasn't until Riddin, soaked with sweat and rain, limped through the doors and into the vast throne room that he could hear the crowd inside.

Khad dwarves churned like a sea of red and black, flooding out of the dozens of doorways that connected the throne room to the rest of the Rock. Stairs to either side led to the balconies and siege weapons above, while ahead, four rows of giant chiseled columns ran the length of the room—split down the center by a smooth walkway that was kept clear of clamoring dwarves by armored soldiers who lined it.

As Riddin made his way down the aisle, Aezik in step behind him, the gathered Khad family quieted to a whisper that first followed, then preceded him. The echoes of conversations grew distant, and the encroaching silence announced Riddin's arrival long before he reached the five shallow steps that led up to the throne.

In a city filled with gems and precious metals, its greatest treasure grew twisted, gnarled, and sunlight-starved behind the Khad throne. The living tree's silver leaves draped down to frame its single occupant who sat half turned toward his daughter's whispers.

Roan Khad's eyes burned as he listened to Vira. His graying, almost white mane of unruly hair and overgrown beard shook with the slight tremor of age. His languid posture suggested apathy before he stiffened at Riddin's approach, and his grip tightened on his most prized possession—a two-handed steel claymore with an elektrum gem set into its golden pommel—that lay across his lap. Throat Cleaver.

"Father." Riddin did his best to kneel. His damaged prosthetic, which was still stuck straight, made the motion difficult and unsteady. When he fell forward onto his hands for support, snickers followed from the crowd. "I come with news."

"So I am told." Roan's deep voice, quiet and cracked with age, reverberated through the halls with the proud power of a king. "Vira tells me an...interesting report. About you and an Unnamed?"

"His Unnamed *lover*," she jeered.

Throat Cleaver crackled as Roan whipped his attention toward her. "You will show Riddin Khad respect while he is my heir!"

Heir reverberated through the room—through the entire Rock, if Riddin had to guess. The attending dwarves' attention never left him, but the oppressive weight of their feelings shifted from disapproval to resentment. It was a weight he was intimately familiar with.

"An Unnamed," Roan said, returning his attention to Riddin. He had brought his volume back under control, but anger still reigned his tone. "Explain."

"He and three others made their way into Yaro's Bar.

Unseen."

"Khad?"

Riddin shook his head. "More Unnamed. One made...a slight against me. Aezik retaliated. Launched him through the bar's front window. The rest of them scattered into—"

"Wouldn't 'ave scattered if it hadn't let 'em!" Viz's familiar voice called from the crowd.

Riddin glanced back to see the dwarf pressed up against the central walkway, favoring his left foot with his arm in a sling. Fury lanced Roan's face as he looked for the disturbance, but Riddin spoke before his father could find the source of his anger.

"The others fled into Prazed territory," Riddin said. "Before *anyone* could pursue them."

"Yet the fourth? The one your giant 'launched through the bar's front window'? What of him?" Riddin took a breath, ready to speak, but Roan held up his hand. "A poor question. Your sister has informed me what became of him. My question should be: *Why* didn't you kill him yourself?"

"No dwarf deserves to die simply for being nameless."

"Hmm. One of your *laws*?"

The word earned ire-filled scoffs from the gathered Khad.

Once again, Roan didn't wait for an answer. "You admit the Unnamed launched a slight against you. Was that not reason enough for death? Surely there is a place in your laws for sense. Or did you, my son, find...*forgiveness* in your heart?"

There was a power behind being king. A power that made

dwarves bend their will and sacrifice themselves for the king's protection. That made even the most stubborn dwarf listen to the king's command. A power to make words mean whatever the king wished.

And with the voice of a king, Roan could inject any word he chose with enough venom—enough hatred—that it couldn't be mistaken for anything but a swear. *Forgiveness* was one such word.

"No," Riddin said. "Not forgiveness. Curiosity."

When his father didn't turn Riddin's *curiosity* into one of his swears, he continued.

"The Unnamed dwarves—both the one now dead and the three who fled—had colors. Armbands. Dyed green with copper. When I questioned the dwarf, he told me he was *not* Unnamed—"

"Then who?" Roan spat the question, anger flooding his voice with an edge of...anticipation? He leaned forward with hunger in his wild eyes, and blue lightning twitched down Throat Cleaver's blade as it shifted in his lap. "I have not given any Unnamed bastards my namesake in over a century, so who has broken our truce, boy? Durza or Prazed?"

"Neither," Riddin said, speaking loud enough for the entire hall. "The dwarf claimed the name Tharkar."

"Tharkar..." Roan's voice trailed as he seemed to retreat into his mind in search of the Old Dwarvish meaning.

Riddin didn't wait for him to find it.

"The Disowned, father. It's a children's story. *Vor Nret.*

Disowned of his name, Vor took the name Tharkar and returned. As king."

Silent tension caught the throne room's breath.

It was broken by Roan Khad's rock-shaking laugh as it echoed through the assembly.

"Ha! There hasn't been a new name under the mountain in two hundred years—two hundred years *today*. Not since the very war that put me on this throne. And now you say an Unnamed has reached into a myth to claim one? When Durza and Prazed are nipping at their borders—*our* borders?" Roan drifted back into his throne, hefted Throat Cleaver with surprising strength, and admired the lightning that danced across its edge in the light. "Tell me, then, Riddin. Who is this heroic myth riling our Unnamed? Did the *Tharkar* Vira killed tell you his namesake?"

"He did." Riddin took a deep, tense breath before letting the words tumble from his mouth. "He said Anezendir was his king."

Any mirth in the room died with Riddin's claim. Despite the thousands gathered, only the pattering rain could be heard as it hit the ground outside and gently trickled into the filling aquifer far above them.

His father's rage was betrayed by the tremor of his shaking muscles, and when he spoke, that rage honed his voice to a whisper. "Anezendir? *King*? The only kings under this mountain were born from the blood of war, and Anezendir *the Unnamed* is not one of them. He will never be one of them!"

"I don't believe—"

Riddin's retort was cut short by Throat Cleaver's arcing swing. The blade sank six inches into the stone floor at his father's feet with a thunderous crash. His father stood against the blade, using it like a staff to propel himself up onto trembling legs, unsteady with age. The gathered Khad—those who despised Riddin's born weakness—let out awed gasps and whispers.

Riddin tried not to resent them for it. He studied the ground and took a deep, shaking breath, then released it.

It didn't help.

Roan's measured words swept through the hall. "Little Anez wants to play king then? Fine. Then I shall play my part as assassin."

Panic leapt through Riddin's chest. "Father, I don't—"

"Let all of Khad hear me!" his father said, raising his voice to address every dwarf in attendance. "I make an offer to you, my family: Flood Mordkin's streets—the conclave's sirens be damned—and deliver Anezendir the Unnamed's head and his *fucking broken crown* to me for one pound of processed elektrum! What say you?"

A pause swept through the throne room. Palpable apprehension built in the hearts of the gathered dwarves while fear built in Riddin's at the sound of the Old Words, the unbreakable contract his father had just offered to the entire Khad family.

One pound of processed elektrum.

The room erupted. Dwarves, civilians and soldiers alike, threw themselves one over another as they scrambled out of the throne room's grinding stone doors and back into Mordkin. Some stayed behind—the few not motivated by greed or too weak to compete—but the streets would soon be filled with dwarves in red and black ready to sweep, search, and slaughter any Unnamed they could find.

On the day of the conclave, violence would bathe the streets.

Riddin hoisted himself forward onto his feet as the clamor died around them. "What have you done?"

Vira stood next to their father, her scowl threatening an attack that was only waylaid by Aezik's hefted war hammer.

"I've set a price on an Unnamed's head," Roan said. "Anezendir should be proud. I haven't done so in decades."

"You know what this will do," Riddin said. "You've given every Unnamed—whether they claim Tharkar or not—a death sentence. The family will feel justified in murdering any they come across in their pursuit—"

"They *are* justified!" Roan yanked Throat Cleaver out of the ground with a grunt and descended the shallow steps. Lightning traced branching paths across the stone as he hefted his unsteady, aging body to Riddin. He clasped a rough hand on the nape of Riddin's neck and pulled him close. His next words were a powerful whisper. "The Unnamed are a nuisance to this city, Riddin. They siphon our water, soil our streets, and steal our food. They are broken and disorganized—but united under any name, they would become a scourge."

"Then we should extend a truce." Riddin tried to pull away, but it seemed his father's age hadn't yet weakened his grip. "They came looking for me on the day of the conclave for a *reason*. If they're as much of a threat as you say, they deserve a seat at the table"—he looked toward his sister—"not a knife to their throats."

"They deserve what every family too weak to earn their name under the mountain deserved when we fought for Mordkin," Roan said. "They deserve death."

"That was two hundred years ago. We don't have to be that way anymore." He looked into his father's gray eyes and saw his age. His determination. "Krest below, Father. He's your son."

"Anezendir is *not* my son!" Roan screamed. His rage echoed through the nearly empty throne room, the few soldiers guarding the entrance and those standing sentinel at the siege weapons the only dwarves who remained to absorb it.

Whether through effort or exhaustion, Roan reigned in his temper. When he spoke again, his voice was quiet. Thoughtful, though no less intense.

"Anezendir is not my son. Not anymore." He looked back up the five shallow steps to the throne Vira now leaned against. "I stripped him of my name because he was too *weak* to do what is *necessary* to be named king—despite whatever he may call himself now." He squeezed his grip on Riddin's nape as he turned back toward his son. "Despite your...inadequacies of birth, I still thought you a better heir than Anezendir *ever* was."

Over Roan's shoulder, Riddin watched Vira squirm, rage robbing her of her scowl.

"But I am still left wondering if you are able to fulfill that responsibility. Did I do the right thing in sparing your life—in naming you heir over your sister? Or is my remaining son still too weak?"

"No!" Riddin barked. Then spoke more deliberately. "No."

"Hmm... We'll see."

Roan released his grip on Riddin's nape with a throw, and the force sent him stumbling backward. He would have fallen if not for Aezik's strong, immovable body stepping up behind him to steady him.

"In two hours, I will be meeting with Avash and Undol on the bronze," Roan said. He swung his crackling sword around to point it directly at Riddin's chest. "And you will join me."

"M-me?" Riddin said.

"*Him*?" Vira snapped.

"Yes." Roan gave her an intense glare that pushed her several steps away from the throne. He then turned his attention back to Riddin. "You. I need to show Durza and Prazed what my successor has to offer. And with the Unnamed threatening us with chaos—with or without Anezendir—well...you've always wanted to propose *unity*, haven't you?"

"Father, I-I didn't think you cared for—"

"Perhaps it's time for Mordkin's families to know what my…chosen heir is willing to do for this city. They must learn to respect the next Khad monarch when the time comes, and"—a wicked grin split Roan Khad's white-bearded face—"who knows how long *I'll* live?"

The whole city was in turmoil. Slaughter called against the Unnamed, stress on the tenuous peace that had surrounded Mordkin since it was established two hundred years ago, and now an acknowledgment of his encroaching age.

And yet Riddin's father was smiling.

"I…" Riddin swallowed. The bronze. A chance to meet the monarchs of the other families—to sue for peace—weighed against the reality that Khad were now looking for blood in the streets. Could he really ignore that? Could he—

"I make an offer to you, Riddin Khad," Roan said, cutting through his thoughts with the echo of another contract. "Your attendance on the bronze on this two hundredth conclave for a meeting between monarchs, and your voice at the table. What say you?"

This was it then. If he accepted the Old Words, he would finally be able to advocate for peace between the families. Real peace. Not the tenuous stalemate of the last two centuries.

Except he would be uniting them against the tens of thousands of Unnamed whose only crime was being nameless. Accept, and he condemned those Unnamed to their deaths. Deny, and he would be disinherited, and his dream of a united Mordkin would be washed away.

But maybe...maybe there was another way...

"I accept, Father," Riddin said. "When the time arrives, I'll meet with you and the other monarchs on the bronze."

"*Excellent*," his father breathed.

A plan less than half formed pieced itself together in Riddin's mind. His hip aching, he turned and walked away from the throne and through one of the many doors along the vast room's walls that led deeper into Khad Rock, Aezik in tow.

He had two hours.

* * *

KHAD ROCK'S HALLWAYS spread out like arteries leading away from the throne room at its heart. They wound and connected and split in an organized chaos that Riddin could only navigate because it was his home.

Eventually, he found his room at the end of a shallow, spiraling hallway. It wasn't much, a closet really. Well, *literally*. A small bedroll that reached from one end of the room to the other had been stuffed along the far wall, an unlit elektrum lamp stood over a desk filled with tinkerer's tools, and some moldy food on royal wooden plates he had forgotten to clean were a testament to the room's privacy that he valued so much.

It wasn't the room of an heir. There were no ornate wood carvings, lavish furniture, nor delicate bed that drowned Riddin in its softness. That room was higher up in the Rock. His brother's room, given to Riddin only seven years ago. No, this was the room Riddin had found and chosen to keep hidden decades ago for one simple reason: the stone hatch hidden beneath his bedroll.

He swung the hatch open, and the familiar smell of stale sweat and stone dust wafted up to greet him. He smiled despite his looming appointment. He would need to be on the bronze in two hours, but there were things he had to take care of before then.

Riddin sat at the hole's steep decline that led down into the earth and then looked over at Aezik. The giant had stopped just on the other side of the doorway's threshold as though to give him privacy, which made his smile deepen.

"Come on then," he said. "And close the hatch when you follow."

With that, he jumped into the hole. Sliding against rough-hewn stone, he was grateful for his prosthetic's inability to feel pain.

Until, that is, a protruding rock caught the edge of the knife wound Vira had carved into it. His metal leg tore beneath him, and he lurched forward. He brought his arms up to slam into the ceiling before his head cracked against it and then brought them forward as the ground rushed up to meet him at the end of the hole.

Riddin's tough dwarven skin was uncut by the fall, but looking down at his leg, he was met with a long tear of jagged metal that flared out like crooked teeth. The cracked and bent inner mechanisms told him that if his prosthetic hadn't been broken before, it would have been now.

"Great..."

The hatch above closed with a grinding thud, followed by Aezik's heavy form thumping down next to Riddin.

In the privacy of the underground tunnels, Aezik offered a hand down to him, and he accepted, allowing the giant to pull him to his feet. His people were made for the darkness, so he could see Aezik's quizzical glance, even in the absence of light.

"I'm fine," Riddin said. "Besides, we were going to Orin's anyway. Now, he'll have a project."

Together, the two walked through the abandoned tunnels beneath the city.

When Riddin's ancestors had found this mountain, it had been the most metal and mineral rich in the world. What was now Mordkin had begun as a mine—strategically cut and excavated for decades, creating a labyrinth of interconnected passageways.

But that had changed when Roan Khad had found the deposit of elektrum he had built his Rock upon. The mines expanded, hollowing the mountain in search of more of that precious gem. Dwarves chose to carve homes into the rocks rather than wasting time venturing in and out of the mountain in hopes of finding their powerful fortunes and cutting their names into history. In the end, Durza had found ignium, Prazed had found disingot, and the other families were killed in the war that followed.

Today, the veins of the precious gems and metals had been mined dry for more than a century—long before Riddin was even born. Most of those tunnels had become Mordkin's streets and homes above, their mined resources now opulent decorations that lined the entire city. But there were many others that had been abandoned, and the most cramped, unprofitable tunnels were forgotten beneath everyone's feet. They ran beneath the entire city in a dense maze filled with dead ends and interconnected pathways.

Riddin had only found the tunnels because of his need to explore as a child—a need to escape the dwarves who beat and scarred him. He visited them often, mapping them out in his mind and connecting their secret exits to the city above. It was here, hidden and safe from a world that hated him, that he had found his love for this city.

It was also where he had found Orin.

The path Riddin and Aezik were following abruptly ended at a perfectly cut wooden door reinforced with metal that sparked blue lightning. Riddin stopped a few feet away, safe from the elektrum-powered security he knew all too well. He didn't need to knock.

A telescopic brass lens extended down from the ceiling above the door with a series of sharp, distinct clicks. Riddin tilted his head, looking up to meet the smooth amber lens with a smirk, as it studied him.

And studied him.

And studied him.

The twisting, shifting movements from the lens kept pulling Riddin in and out of focus as though trying to find him. After a full minute of this, Riddin's smirk fell into annoyance.

"I told him to put a light on that thing," he said.

The lens stopped rotating, then recoiled abruptly back into the wall. A series of loud scrapes and grinds betrayed the locks falling away on the other side of the wooden door and, finally, the blue lightning ceased arcing across the metal reinforcements. Riddin stepped forward to open the door, and the first warm light he had seen in nearly a mile of unlit tunnels filtered through the door's widening cracks and into the dust-filled haze.

The room was actually a larger-than-normal intersection in the tunnels, where four separate pathways intersected. Each of the eight paths was closed off by its own tightly fit, electrified door. Muffled, tinny sounds of the city blared through the speaker affixed to the ceiling, connected to the hidden listeners Riddin had helped place in the streets above. The room dropped two steep steps into a sunken center, in the middle of which ran an elektrum-powered forge. Lightning ran through a bed of tight tungsten coils until they glowed a bright orange that bathed the room in heat.

An old man—a real full-sized human—sat sweating at his workbench on the other side of the room. The low ceilings, mined for dwarven heights, had placed a permanent hunch on his shoulders after all his years down in the tunnels. His long, slender fingers twiddled away tirelessly at something Riddin couldn't see from the doorway, and he turned his head to look at Riddin without stopping his work.

"I thought that was you," the old man said.

The room's glowing light reflected in Orin's fractured, amber-lensed goggles like a bug's eyes. Combined with the seal-tight respirator affixed to his mouth and nose, his expression was impossible to read. Though Riddin had always associated the way his thick gray eyebrows furrowed over his goggles as a passive, permanent anger. Or offense.

"Well, you don't ever come just to chat anymore," Orin said. His respirator gave his deep, gruff voice the same tinny ring as the speaker. "I trust something shit out?"

Riddin walked toward the workbench, his unresponsive prosthetic nearly sending him into Orin's forge. As Aezik followed him inside, the artificer leaned forward to his wall of levers and flipped one back into the up position—closing, locking, and resecuring the door with elektrum.

"Peacekeeper didn't work." Riddin drew the gun from his hip and set it on the table. Then pulled several of Orin's tools over and got to work unscrewing the casing. "I pulled the trigger four times. Nothing. Not even a misfire. I think it has something to do with the actuator changes we made."

"The removal, you mean," Orin said.

He nodded.

Now that he was at the bench, he spared a glance at what

Orin had been working on. The grip, the barrel, the familiar inner mechanisms exposed outside of the weapon's frame. Another gun. Interesting.

Orin, of course, didn't move to help him. Instead, he stared down at Riddin's side as though he was looking through the workbench and at his prosthetic.

"It's fine," Riddin said.

"*Looks* fine. If 'isn't working at all' is fine. Looks great even."

"I'm more worried about the gun."

"Hmm, trust me. I know." Orin stood and came around to Riddin's side. With a series of quick expert twists that Riddin didn't bother to protest, he pulled Riddin's prosthetic free from the hip and heaved it up onto the workbench with a resounding crash. "The young are always more worried about their damning toys than their health."

Riddin's driver slipped off a screw and struck the table. "We're the same age, Orin."

"I'm human. The years age me differently."

"Not too differently." Riddin nodded to Orin's own prosthetic, a simple foot replacement with an ankle joint that started well below the knee.

Orin gave an acknowledging nod as he worked.

As Riddin unscrewed Peacekeeper's final connector, he pointed at Orin's other project with the tip of his driver. "Another gun?" he asked. "I thought we agreed Peacekeeper would be the only one."

Orin gave a halfhearted wave, wrench in hand. "Not *another* one. A replacement. You mentioned the actuator change? Well, we've strayed so far from your designs that we were bound to run into problems. Honestly, we should have expected as much considering where your concept originated from. Turning something that large into something this small was always going to be a shitting challenge.

"That"—he pointed across Riddin's face and at the in-progress gun—"is meant to solve those problems. All of them. Smaller frame, more efficient coil mechanism, and a few other...improvements. I've even found a way around our priming problem."

"Really?" Riddin asked. There was a delay between pulling Peacekeeper's trigger and the shot actually being fired. It was necessary to allow the charge to build up safely, but they had been trying to find a way to reduce it for months. "What's the solution?"

"You'll see," Orin said. "There're still some kinks to iron out, but it won't have nearly as many scars as your current prototype. And speaking of scars, it seems you'll need to add one more."

With Peacekeeper's outer casing removed, Riddin stared at the mechanism inside the gun's hilt. While Orin had diagnosed the problem immediately—without even *looking*—he had to swing over the large magnifying glass attached to a spring arm. He assessed each component top to bottom, careful to use an insulated tool to prod around the small elektrum gem set into the gun's core until he found the problem himself.

"There's too much space between the trigger and the elektrum coil," Riddin said. "The pin doesn't even reach the spin wheel anymore. I might be able to—"

He turned to grab the spool of low-melt metal that Orin kept on his desk for quick soldering, but the old man—head still buried in repairing his leg—was already holding it out to him.

"Thanks," he grumbled. He snatched the spool from Orin's hand, turned, and pulled a hot-tipped steel rod from the forge behind him. He brought the solder and steel over the gun and filled the gap with melting conductive filler. It wasn't a perfect solution, and it was far from pretty, but that was what prototypes were for.

This just needed to work. Let Orin worry about pretty.

"What did you do to this thing, Riddin?" Orin asked as he finished with his leg. "The gears were bent and gouged, and the hydraulics were drained—not to mention the plating!"

"I...fell," he lied.

"Fine. Don't tell me. I'm just your only shitting friend in this whole fuck city."

Aezik shifted forward, but Orin waved him off.

"Excepting the walking column of stone, of course. My point is"—Orin knelt by Riddin's side and slid his prosthetic back into his hip with a click—"you should be more careful. Life's dangerous down here, especially for *krevtish* like us."

"Really?" Riddin said. "I had no idea."

Orin swatted away Riddin's sarcasm as he stood—as much as he could with the low ceiling—and walked to the wall littered with tools and scraps of all shapes and sizes. It was a disorganized chaos, the contents of which Riddin only knew half of.

"I couldn't fix it completely," Orin said as he rifled through the wall's contents. "Should bend now, at least at the ankle, but you won't have a full range of motion until I can take a good, long look. It might even require a full replacement."

"Still better than the last one," Riddin said, returning to his soldering.

"If you keep 'falling,' you'll end up back in the last one. Here we are..." He shuffled to Riddin's side at the workbench. "I'll start working on a temporary but functional replacement so I can take a better look at that leg in the future. After the business with the updated gun design, of course. Until then..."

He struck the workbench with a long, polished stick made of ornate wood that sent a *crack* through the room and stole Riddin's attention. It had a large knot on top for Riddin's hand and a textured metal stopper on the bottom to avoid slipping against the stones.

"No," Riddin said.

"It's only temporary—"

"I'm done using a cane. I don't need it! That's why we built this leg in the first place."

"And now that leg is damn broken. You need it, Riddin."

Fueled with frustration and anger, Riddin pushed himself off the chair and strode around the forge. He walked with purpose—arms held in wide defiance with a triumphant strut—but Orin had been right. While he could move considerably better than before, the limited range of motion was a severe hindrance. The result was him nearly falling, repeatedly, into the heated tungsten forge, saved only by several lucky stumbles. By the time he finished his walk, embarrassment had chased away his anger.

"Please, Orin," he said. "I can't afford to look weak. Not now."

"Now?" Orin paused his work—having taken up Peacekeeper's repair once more—and looked at him through faceted amber lenses. "What's happening now?"

He tried to hold Orin's gaze with a determined expression, eyes fierce and jaw clenched. The result was a room that swam with silence, aside from the elektrum-powered hum that kept the forge glowing and the doors secure. But Orin's resolve could outmatch even the most stubborn of dwarves. In the end, Riddin's will folded, and he told the old man everything, starting with the Tharkar at the bar.

"Has Roan Khad lost his *mind*?" Orin snarled. "A *pound* of elektrum? What happened to offering gold as a damning reward?"

"Gold?" Riddin asked, but he waved him off.

"Wood. Shit, *seeds* if he was desperate. But *elektrum*? That would send the entire Khad family stomping through the city, eager for blood."

"And it has."

"You included, I'll wager!" His voice grew low and disapproving. "A pound of elektrum would go a long way for you, wouldn't it? Suppose you're wanting to collect, then?"

"What? No. Orin, what good would that do me? I know where the elektrum stores are." Riddin had found them during his exploration of the tunnels as well. "If I needed it, I could take it. Not to mention they're my *inheritance*. I'll possess all of it soon enough, so why should I care about a single pound?"

Orin gave a hesitant nod and skeptical grunt before turning his frustrated hands back to Peacekeeper's repair.

"I *am* going to search for Anez," Riddin said. "But not to kill him. I'm going to warn him."

The idea had struck Riddin in the throne room, but it was the long walk through the abandoned tunnels that had given him enough time to think over the specifics. Orin's brows furrowed over his amber lenses as he continued.

"The Unnamed, the Tharkar, whatever they want to call themselves—they're boiling, Orin. Not *threatening* to boil. They're already spilling over. Into alleys, homes, bars—and the families? Khad has been beating the Unnamed back like animals for decades, and the others aren't any better. None of them care to look at what's *really* causing the problems in this city. And now?

If a Khad—if *anyone*—kills the one the dwarf the Unnamed have chosen as a *king*?"

"It will be...messy."

There was a distance to Orin's voice that Riddin couldn't quite understand. Perhaps it was because this city wasn't his the same way it was Riddin's.

"It will be *chaos*," Riddin said. "I'm not about to let another war like the one that gave birth to my father's reign divide and kill Mordkin—not when I've almost inherited the power to change it. I'm going to go to Anez and convince him to stand aside. Ask him to renounce the name Tharkar and flee to Durza or Prazed's Mordkin. Either is safer for him now."

"Why would Anezendir agree to that?" Orin spun in his seat with an exacerbated sigh. "He's calling himself a king under Khad rule *now*. Self-preservation doesn't seem like a motivating factor for him."

"I don't believe Anez meant offense. I know him; he wants to protect this city. He hates how my father rules just as much as I do. He'll accept my offer because it's for the good of Mordkin." Riddin took a shaking breath and stood as tall as he could. "And because I'll recognize the Tharkar name myself when I'm king—w*ithout* the need for bloodshed. Anez wants peace. He always has. He'll agree to this, I know it."

He watched Orin's unreadable face as the old man seemed to consider his argument. He was almost sure he had convinced him he didn't need the cane. Until Orin reached up to the table, grabbed the wooden stick, and thrust it toward him again.

"Orin, I can't—"

"Fucking *take* the cane." Orin's voice trembled. "You're right. You need to present a strong front to someone if you're hoping to trade a peaceful today for a promised tomorrow—a really fucky idea by the way, but I understand it's your only real bargaining chip." He pushed the cane forward, jamming the point into Riddin's chest. "What *you* need to understand is you'll present a far stronger front if you're not falling on your damn-shit face while you're doing it. *Take the cane*!"

Riddin wanted to deny him again. To hesitate. To argue. But what else could he do? Orin...never got this upset. He cared about this more than any project or design they had ever worked on together. He cared about Riddin.

So, Riddin reached forward and took the cane. "Thank you, Orin."

"Good." Orin spun back around to the workbench, calling an end to the conversation.

Despite his reluctance, Riddin was grateful for the cane. It offered him stability and allowed him to evenly distribute his weight, alleviating the chronic pain in his hip that had become aggravated by his uneven gait.

He made his way to the slantmost-facing door out of Orin's workshop with Aezik lumbering in tow, his war hammer draped across his shoulders. They waited as Orin flipped one of the levers at his workbench, disconnecting the elektrum security and unlocking the door with a clang and a creak. Then with a deep breath, Riddin opened the door into the dark tunnels.

"Wait."

Riddin turned toward the voice, expecting to see Orin at his workbench. Instead, the old man towered over him, slouched and looming like an old-growth tree. Before he could fall back in surprise, Orin grabbed his wrist and dropped the fully reassembled Peacekeeper into his hand.

"In my experience, peace is an excellent goal, but a damny backup plan." Orin's expression was unreadable beneath the mask, but his tone was laced with worry. "If Anezendir doesn't give you a choice... Well, you'll be glad to have the option. Even if the shitting giant fights all your fights."

"Thank you, Orin." Riddin slid Peacekeeper into the sheath at his hip. His fingers lingered on the hand-warmed metal. Smiling, he placed his hand on the old man's arm. "Do me a favor while I'm gone. Try and get better at swearing."

"Not my fault your language is so fuck hard," Orin said, but Riddin could hear the smile in his voice. And he heard when it fell, too. "Do you even know where to look for Anezendir? Mordkin is a big city. Or so these tunnels lead me to believe."

"I have an idea," he said, then turned to enter the darkness of the familiar tunnels.

Mordkin *was* a big city—but only for those who didn't know it like Riddin did. If all he had to go on was his knowledge of these tunnels and the fact Anezendir was, at the very least, in slantward Khad territory, it would have been enough. But that wasn't all Riddin had to go on. He knew exactly where to find the Tharkar king.

After all, his brother had sent him an invitation.

* * *

WHILE EVERY DWARF under Khad Rock shared a namesake—were family—Roan Khad only had two children: Riddin, his *krevtish* son who should have died as a child because of his deformity but who Roan had chosen instead to save, and Vira, his daughter who had not only been given his name but had been adopted fully in the wake of her parents' assassinations.

However, until seven years ago, there had been a third Khad child.

Anezendir was the oldest of them. When their mother had died, he had been the one to teach Riddin how to walk, talk, and live under a dwarven society who saw him as less than worthy of the life Roan had allowed him to keep. Through him, Riddin had been encouraged to think, to design, and to tinker—not because he was a designer or tinkerer himself, but because of his belief in Riddin's potential. A belief he had extended to every dwarf in Mordkin when he had been heir.

Even before taking the throne, he was always a dwarf set on peace with the power and influence of a king. Riddin had been excited for the day he would inherit. The day their father's hold of the past would be replaced by their vision of the future.

Yet seven years ago, Roan had disinherited Anezendir. Unnamed him. Abandoned him to the streets of Mordkin without a hint of explanation other than he was king, and he could do as he wished.

In an instant, the dwarves Anezendir had become king to in all but name turned away from him. Khad—his family—treated him the same as any other Unnamed, stripping him of his colors and beating him out of Khad Rock until he was with the rest of the filth in slantward Mordkin.

Despite the disdain Riddin faced from every other dwarf in Mordkin, Roan had named Riddin his new heir. While Riddin still struggled to make those around him recognize his new station, it seemed not even becoming Unnamed could stop his brother from becoming a king.

As Riddin and Aezik continued down Mordkin's slant, the tunnels under the city grew shallow and hot. Sweat trickled off Riddin's bald head, and Aezik was forced to stoop down with the dropping ceiling that eventually grew too low to continue. Riddin found an exit that fed into one of the many abandoned homes above, and Aezik followed up after him and closed the tunnel entrance with the only thing Mordkin had in abundance: stone.

Where hillward Mordkin was grand, with buildings and towers that scraped or even merged with the city's ceiling, slantward Mordkin was a collection of slot canyon gutters. The rain that fell throughout the city gathered and funneled through the long, narrow streets, creating small rivers that trickled and weathered grooves into the stone. The buildings were straight cut and half finished, rough-hammered gold and silver barely scaffolding partially carved houses that had been left abandoned when the plains had failed.

As the two traveled farther down, the thermal vents just beneath the street's surface—the same vents that had stopped the mining of the tunnels centuries ago—made the flowing water steam and blanket the streets in a thin, low fog. Refuse and waste gathered along the edges of the flowing rivers, carried down by water and gravity through a city built on a permanent decline. The more water that evaporated, the more of what was left behind solidified into a brownish-green sediment paste that hardened to the baking rock and the worse the smell became.

Every inch of the street held Unnamed in its flanks. Some tried to stay away from the stinking waste they were forced to live with, but older Unnamed were resigned to their state of perpetual filth, their clothes and skin stained with their long years of forced squalor.

Descending deeper, Riddin recognized the trouble he and Aezik were in. Many Unnamed wore green Tharkar armbands, and they all took notice of Riddin's and Aezik's swirling red and black clothing that denoted them as Khad. While they never tried to stop Riddin and Aezik, the Tharkar shifted and circled along the outskirts like bats over a rotting meal.

Riddin's knuckles bled white as he gripped Peacekeeper's

hilt. Next to him, Aezik's muscles tensed as he hefted his war hammer, ready for one wrong move from their followers—that thankfully never came. Even if Riddin hadn't already known where Anezendir was, he had a feeling these Tharkar, who were moving to block any exit back hillward, would have led him to the dwarf themselves.

At the slantward edge of Mordkin, the decline ended in a gutter that carried what little water was left to the edges of the mountain and out through slotted grooves that dumped refuse down the mountain's slopes. Beyond the gutter, in a large flat field, was what now remained of Mordkin's greatest hope: the plains.

The thermal vents beneath the stone meant that Riddin's ancestors couldn't dig any lower. However, it was thought that the natural heat would be ideal for farming—something the city desperately needed. The ground had been mined flat and excavated. Mineral-rich stone had been ground and churned into fine soil. Dwarf-made stalactites were carved in regular intervals, controlling the drip of filtered water brought down from the melting ice and rainfall on the mountain above.

It worked too. For about fifteen years, the plains fed all of Mordkin.

Then, before Riddin had even been born, the earthquake had come. Aside from minor damages, the city itself was left unaffected. However, the thermal vents beneath the plains had been ruptured, and where gentle warmth had once blown, magma flowed. The soil was dried and robbed of its nutrients, and no matter how hard any dwarf tried, nothing could grow.

Now, the stalactites dripped onto scorching sand, evaporating the water the moment it hit the ground. The churning magma beneath the stone sent the entire plains into a rolling sway, and the dunes that had once been soil shifted and rolled like small, tumbling waves.

Which was why, when Anezendir had first brought Riddin here, he had called it a lake.

The only lake in Mordkin.

Dwarves could barely survive the heat of the plains, even with their thick skin and efficient lungs. But today, thirteen dwarves, all dressed in green-dyed leather, haphazard metal, and ragged cloth, stood around a table barely visible from the shore.

Growing nerves crawling under his skin, Riddin looked up, hoping to find his courage set into the ceiling. However, there had been no reason for his ancestors to line quartz into the purpose-made stalactites above. There were no stars in slantward Mordkin.

One of the Tharkar at the table spotted him by the lake's edge and nudged another, prompting them to turn around. The dwarf saw him, then approached, moving across the swaying plains like they had been born for it. He squinted at them through the hot, shimmering air, and his body tensed with hesitation as he recognized the unfamiliar dwarf.

Anezendir was built wide. As a Khad, it had made him

thick and strong like a statue, but the life of an Unnamed had seen him malnourished into a lean, wide frame that made his clothes—thick leather and cloth with steel armored accents—billow in the humid breeze. His beard and hair, once well-kempt and short, were overgrown into uneven wisps that swirled in the rising heat. They framed his face with a strange wildness.

When Anezendir was close enough, his face burst at the seams with his smile, his dry skin wrinkled with an age only earned by hardship. "Riddin!"

Relief flooded through him, relaxing his body. And after seven long years of not seeing his brother, Riddin couldn't help but return that smile. "Anez!"

Riddin stepped forward. Where Anezendir moved across the lapping sand with practiced grace, his steps were careful and uneasy. His cane slipped as it failed to find solid ground, and Aezik discreetly steadied him by his arm, letting him stumble up onto the swaying plains without appearing incompetent.

He looked back to thank the giant, but found Aezik's face drained of color, even in the heat. In the thirty years he had known Aezik, the giant had never once looked the way he did now. Hesitant. Worried. He had seen Aezik barrel into danger without a second thought so many times that he had never considered there would be something to give the giant pause. That there was anything that could shake him.

But here, on the shores of the swaying plains, eyes locked

on the unsteady ground that shifted beneath them, Aezik looked afraid.

Riddin nodded, signaling to Aezik that it was okay for him to stay on the shore if that was where he felt more comfortable. Besides, he wouldn't need protection where Anezendir was concerned. The same relief that had relaxed Riddin's muscles seemed to relax Aezik's at the acknowledgment, and Aezik took up position as a sentry on the edge of the plains. Alone, Riddin continued his unsteady walk forward.

With any luck, his cane wouldn't slip again.

When the two brothers met—substantially closer to the shore than to the table near the lake's center—Anezendir pulled Riddin into a hard embrace.

"It does me good to see you!" Anezendir pulled away, held him at arm's length, and looked him up and down. "Let me take a look... Krest below, you've grown. Well, not much. They must still feed you like shit!" His gaze lingered on Riddin's hip for a moment before flashing back up into his eyes. "At least they dress you well, eh?"

"I dress myself actually," Riddin said. "I could teach you, if you like."

"Watch yourself!" But Anezendir's smile broadened. "They still wasting your talents at the aquifer's gates?"

So, Anezendir didn't know. Of course he didn't know.

"N-no," Riddin started. "Actually, I'm—"

"Good!" He wrapped his arm around Riddin's shoulder

and ushered him deeper into the plains. "I didn't raise you to use that brain of yours just to have it rot on the top of that wall." He nodded at Riddin's hip. At Peacekeeper. "Looks to me like you're cultivating your talents instead, eh?"

"Trying to." Riddin needed to focus the conversation. He didn't know how much of a lead he had gained on the other Khad seeking his father's bounty, but even after traveling by the tunnels, it couldn't have been much. "Listen, Anez. I came here to—"

"I know why you're here." His broad smile faltered. "I...I wasn't sure you'd come, if we're being honest here, Riddin. I sent you a message, and you killed my messenger. I figured I had your answer."

"*Vira* killed him. Not me." Though, admittedly, he had tried.

"Hmm... And was Vira the one who launched Tellimaz through a fucking window?"

"Do I look like I could do that? That was Aezik, and he was right to do it after your dwarf insulted me. You can't blame us for that."

"Of course I can't. It never is your fault, is it, Riddin?" Anezendir's words carried an unfamiliar, accusatory sting that vanished with the wave of his hand. "Forget it. None of that matters now. I had hoped to hear the news from Tellimaz, but now you're here yourself. So, your answer is yes, yes?"

"My answer?" Riddin thought back to the exchange on Tri-street. "Anez, all your dwarf did was spit in my face, call you a king, and tell me where to find you. Barely. What is there to answer?"

"Fucking Tellimaz." Anezendir slowed, and his language stiffened as they neared the table, their conversation gaining more ears. "The power in Mordkin is swaying, Riddin. Shifting—like the plains beneath our feet. I've given a name to the nameless."

"I've heard," Riddin said. "Tharkar."

A surge roiled beneath Riddin's feet, forcing him to grab the edge of the table to keep himself from collapsing. The other dwarves effortlessly swayed with the unpredictable plains, their practiced feet steadying them. Even if he'd had two good legs, Riddin wouldn't have been able to stay upright. Not like them.

And he'd been worried the cane would make him look weak.

Pushing himself off the table, Riddin recognized a crude map of Mordkin, complete with its uneven borders and branching streets. Points of interest were placed throughout the city. Most were concentrated around Tri-street and the family Rocks. What they denoted, Riddin could only guess, but the table's purpose—and the purpose of the surrounding dwarves—became very, very clear.

"You're... This is a war table," Riddin said. "You're planning to fight?"

"As is our right!" a dwarf around the table shouted. His beard was long and white, save for the greenish brown stains that gathered it in thick knots. "Names are forged in blood like steel in heat, and Tharkar has yet to go through the crimson flame. Already the Khad king fears us, sending his dogs to bark at our borders, but we are twenty thousand strong. We will not be quelled—not easily, not ever!"

"Twenty...twenty thousand?" How had a new name grown so large under everyone's noses? Or was Khad simply the last to find out?

"And our numbers grow by the hour." Anezendir shot the outspoken dwarf a silencing glare. "The Unnamed are rallying behind us, claiming my namesake and our mission. Though admittedly...we are still at a disadvantage when comparing our numbers to the families."

"Numbers? Anez, how do you plan to face elektrum? Or ignium? Or disiplate? With steel? The last dwarves who tried that were slaughtered two hundred years ago!"

"We'll 'ave elektrum of our own," another dwarf said. Her brown eyes narrowed toward him. "Long as you follow through on your end o' our deal."

Their...deal? Riddin turned to find Anezendir with both hands on the table, eyes clenched shut as though trying to find peace in a current that had swept him away. When had his brother become so...old?

"Anez?" Riddin asked.

Anezendir took in a deep breath, and with an almost practiced silence, the Tharkar around the table turned their attention to their king before he even released it. "Know this," he said, opening his eyes. "We will fight for our namesake, no matter the cost. We will fight, and we will die, and we will be content knowing we've killed at least some of the bastards who have degraded and beaten and robbed us of everything—even our very names.

"But with your help, Riddin..." He looked sidelong at him. "You know where Roan has moved the elektrum stores—I know you do. If you give us that, and if you lend us your mind—that beautiful mind I *know* is stronger than any dwarf under the mountain—we might actually win. Perhaps not against every family but against one. With you at our side, I know we can kill at least one monarch. One who's always underestimated you—underestimated *us*. Together, we can kill Roan Khad." He turned to face Riddin, his aged, determined eyes alive with hopeful fire. "And when we do...I will put you in his place."

The Tharkar erupted with yells and cries of betrayal at Anezendir's final words—his offer—while others defended him. Insults were muttered, fists were thrown, and the heat of the swaying plains grew with the dwarves' rage.

"Enough!" Anezendir shouted.

The infighting ceased.

"Who am I? Some Unnamed dwarf whose words mean less than the gem they are cut on, or am I your *king*?" He pounded his chest as he spoke, his green leather giving a soft thump that somehow carried more weight than if it had been plate armor. "I am Anezendir Tharkar, and *you* are my family now. We will go to war, we will cut our name on Roan Khad's throne, and we will watch him beg for death when we do! But what need have we of that throne after his blood is spilled? When we will have a throne of our own!" He turned back to Riddin. "So, I make an offer to you, Riddin *Khad*—the dwarf I once called brother and would still call my ally: your allegiance in this inevitable war, for a throne at your feet. What say you?"

Riddin stared into his brother's gray eyes as the contract of the Old Words echoed across the swaying plains. His brother, who had taught him how to walk on one leg before he had welded his first prosthetic, who had shown him kindness in a world of hate, and who had always spoken of bringing peace to Mordkin—not just a tenuous truce between families, but *real peace*.

And with a sinking heart, he recognized that the Anezendir before him wasn't that dwarf anymore. But maybe, beneath that rage and fury on Anezendir's snarling face, that dwarf was still there. Somewhere.

All Riddin had to do was find him.

"I came here to offer a different path." Riddin's voice felt weak compared to Anezendir's. Dry and crackly in the heat. He cleared his throat and pushed off the table before continuing to address the entire group. "In Anezendir's place, Roan Khad has named *me* heir."

If Anezendir hadn't known before, he didn't seem to show any sign of surprise.

"He is old," Riddin continued. "Feeble. When he dies, I

will be named Khad's king *without* the need for bloodshed, and when I am, I will recognize the name Tharkar—but only if you choose peace. Here. Now. Forget your plan of attack and move into Prazed or Durza territory before the Khad looking to collect my father's bounty find and kill you."

All eyes turned to Anezendir, Riddin's included, but the Tharkar king's gaze was unyielding. He turned and leaned back against the table, arms crossed and steady in the constant sway. The fierce sidelong silence bored into Riddin, making him take an unsteady step away from the table.

"Anez...please. You know me. You know Mordkin! Is bloodshed *really* what's best when we can achieve your dream of peace—our dream of peace—without it?"

"All we 'ave to do is wait for Roan Khad t' die of 'is own accord!" the second dwarf from earlier shouted. "How long'll 'at be? A year? Ten? Why wait when we could kill 'em and be done with it?"

"Aye," another Tharkar said. "Why continue living under Khad's cruelty when we can do something about it *now*?"

A murmur of agreement rose through the Tharkar, and the heat of the plains continued to rise with their anger. Riddin took another staggering step back from the table, his stomach dropping.

Leaving Aezik behind had been a mistake.

"If you do this, you will be exchanging one cruelty for another," Riddin said. "One that will result in thousands of deaths—tens of thousands! Mordkin will be made weaker for it."

"Perhaps Mordkin deserves to be weakened," Anezendir said, finally speaking. "Like steel. It must be made malleable before it can be shaped."

"And the war against Khad will be our furnace!" a knot-bearded Tharkar shouted.

The others jeered in agreement. Then as though commanded by some unseen voice, all thirteen Tharkar turned on Riddin with flames of fury behind their eyes.

The ground shifted beneath Riddin's cane as he took another unsteady step back, and his cane slipped. He crumbled backward as the wood left his hand, and scorching sand burned his skin as he hit the ground. Heart racing, he scrambled onto his hands and feet, but the ground offered no purchase. The shifting sands of the swaying plains were nothing like the firm stones of the shore so far behind him.

The Tharkar were moving now. They encroached, surrounding him as he dragged himself backward like a wounded animal.

"You're not listening to me!" Riddin pleaded. "I am heir to the Khad throne. When I succeed my father, I'll give you the recognition you seek. I swear!"

"Heirs." Anezendir's voice was laced with a cruelty Riddin had heard from his family before—but never from him. "*Succession*. Do you know how many princes there have been in Mordkin these last two hundred years? Across Khad, Durza, and

Prazed? Seven. One is dead, one is crawling upon the ground in front of me, and five are right here on these plains, looking down at you. None have ever succeeded their throne, and do you want to know why? It's because the title is a lie. There are no princes under the mountain, Riddin. Only kings."

Two of the Tharkar broke from the encroaching pack and stalked closer on either side of Riddin as he scrambled away. They drew crude weapons from hidden folds in their clothes.

Riddin drew Peacekeeper from his hip. He aimed at one. Then at the other. Yet his finger hesitated on the trigger. There was still a chance. There had to be. He needed to try.

"Please don't do this, Anez," Riddin said. "Just give me time. Let me succeed our father, and I'll finally have the power to bring peace to Mordkin like we always talked about! Isn't that what you want? Peace?"

"Once," Anezendir said, "but that was before I learned the truth of this city. The truth behind why Khad, Durza, and Prazed won the war that put them on their thrones, and why they will never cede them. In this city, power cannot be given. It cannot be inherited or earned or passed on. In Mordkin, power must be *taken*."

The two flanking dwarves rushed forward, their thin frames quick and lithe on the hot, shifting sand. The left dwarf inched ahead of her companion and raised her short sword. Desperation and the joy of rage sculpted her face.

Riddin forced his focus on her, finally holding his aim.

With a silent prayer that his repair had worked, he pulled the trigger.

Peacekeeper whirred to life as the firing pin completed the elektrum-metal circuit, and electricity wound itself through the spin coil. The half second that passed as the gun charged its shot brought the attacking dwarf's sword down in a killing blow, and he knew he had been too late. Too late to pull the trigger. Too late to stop Anezendir.

Orin had been right. A promise of peace had been a terrible idea.

And now Riddin would die for it.

A condensed bolt of blue lightning leapt from Peacekeeper's barrel. It electrified the air and filled Riddin's mouth with the taste of plasma in an instant. The shot punched a hole through the cutting dwarf's chest as she slashed. The force of the shot threw Riddin back onto the sand, and his attacker's swing missed his head.

And instead, it found his hand.

Steel cleanly cut through his bottom two fingers before striking Peacekeeper's metal frame. The impact wrenched the gun from his ruined grip, sending it flying across the sand. The Tharkar, her desperation now mixed with surprise instead of joy, collapsed on top of Riddin. Lifeless.

The second dwarf, his one-handed hammer raised above Riddin, paused at the sudden death of his companion. If Riddin had been alone, the Tharkar's moment of hesitation wouldn't have mattered. Trapped beneath the dwarf he had killed and without Peacekeeper, Riddin could do nothing to stop the attacking dwarf from bringing his hammer down.

But in the breath of the dwarf's stunned pause, Aezik's stone-headed war hammer finished its flight through the air and smashed into the second dwarf's head, snapping his neck and sending him flying back onto the sand with the sound of crunching bone.

Aezik himself soon followed, feet unsteady and face pale. He passed Riddin with a quick, assessing glance before returning his attention to where his war hammer had fallen and walking out of sight.

Riddin could hear the second dwarf's dying gasps somewhere in the sand ahead, his mangled mouth and crushed brain trying to resume living after his skull had been split. But his desperate struggle ended after Aezik lifted his war hammer and let it fall back onto the dwarf's head with a silencing squelch that shook the ground. The shouts and screams from the other Tharkar rose over the plains, and the giant charged away from Riddin to meet them.

Finding his strength, Riddin twisted and dragged himself from beneath the dwarf he had killed as the violence he had tried so hard to avoid reverberated around him. His guilt and determination clashed. This was his fault. He needed to stop it.

He was nearly free when his prosthetic snagged on the first dwarf's dead body and halted his progress. Flesh and cloth tangled in the still-jagged metal that had been cut by Vira's dagger, then torn open by his fall in the tunnels. The dead dwarf's body jerked as he pulled, but his efforts only dug the metal deeper into her flesh.

A body sailed over Riddin's head—thrown by Aezik in the giant's fight—and thumped onto the sand a few feet away with a back-breaking snap. Riddin stared at the thrown body, recognizing the sneering dwarf from the table. The one with a knotted, stained beard. Even in death, his face was still contorted with snide hatred.

Then the dwarf's eyes flashed open.

The dwarf pushed himself up by his hands, but his legs refused to move. He let loose a scream that would have rivaled the city's klaxon alarm, and that only seemed to deepen his rage. He fell forward onto his elbows, then set his gaze upon Riddin. A vengeful fire alive in his gray eyes, he crawled forward, dragging his broken body across the sand.

Riddin strained beneath the dead dwarf's weight with renewed fervor, but it was pointless. The jagged metal only sank its teeth deeper. Defenseless, he searched the sands for something—anything.

And found the dead dwarf's short sword not far from where she had fallen.

He hurled himself forward again and again, doubling over as he strained his muscles and used his momentum to stretch for the sword. He managed to brush the pommel, but his hand—missing two fingers and slick with blood—slipped with each desperate grasp.

Until he found the grip between his thumb and forefinger. Until he dragged the sword toward him by the pommel. Until he threw himself forward one last time to grab the hilt and—

Rough hands found Riddin's shoulders and threw him back down onto the sands, the sword slipping impossibly far from his reach. His vision filled with the rageful eyes of the sneering dwarf, whose rough hands slipped from Riddin's shoulders, found his throat, and squeezed with a deadly grip.

Riddin fought to pry his opponent's hands from around his neck, but his blood-soaked fingers continued to betray him. He punched up, but the Tharkar didn't even need to pull away to dodge his pathetic reach.

Everything—the heat of the sand against his back, the sensation of the swaying ground beneath them, and the sounds of Aezik's battle just beyond his sight—it all faded as blood pooled in his ears, and air fought to escape his lungs. He writhed, his fighting turning to desperate flailing beneath the Tharkar's immense weight. Handfuls of crimson-clumped sand poured from between his fingers as he continued hopelessly grasping for the sword he knew was too far away.

Until he found it.

Riddin's hand wrapped around the sword's hilt—a lifeline among the fading chaos. How had it gotten so close to him? It didn't matter. He affirmed his grip—the blade wouldn't slip from his hand again—and swung it up at the dwarf's head with enough force to cut through bone.

The wooden cane snapped in half as it met his opponent's hard head.

Not even dazed, the Tharkar simply laughed and tightened his choking grip. Riddin's vision darkened as he stared at the broken cane in his hand. Its tip was now sharp and jagged. Despite the break, the wood was strong. It wasn't a sword, but...

Body failing, Riddin shook uncontrollably as his arm dropped back down to his side. He forced it straight. He forced it steady.

Then with every ounce of strength he could muster, he stabbed the jagged piece of wood up into the Tharkar's neck.

Surprise replaced the dwarf's sneer, then fled along with the life that now poured red onto Riddin's face and clothes. His grip vanished from Riddin's throat, choosing to grab at the wooden cane that speared his own neck instead.

Riddin pushed the stabbed dwarf to the side, where he easily fell. Free from the deluge of blood, he took in lungful after lungful of rust-tinged air, and the rest of his senses slowly returned as the dwarf next to him died.

The plains burned with the smell of evaporating blood. Propping himself onto his elbows, he saw Tharkar bodies littering the ground, half sunken into the ever shifting sand. Deeper onto the plains, Aezik fought on as the remaining five Tharkar circled him like wolves. He swung his war hammer in wide unsure arcs, while they dashed forward with their swords and hammers, nipping at him with steel that sliced and bruised his flesh before dodging away again.

Desperate, Riddin searched for something—anything he could do to help. If he didn't, Aezik wouldn't just fight to protect Riddin. He would *die*. In his search, he found hope in a glimmer of metal beneath the war table, half buried in the sand like the bodies that surrounded him.

Peacekeeper.

Riddin dropped back down onto his back and jerked himself to the left, forcing his body to twist beneath the snagged weight of the first dwarf he'd killed. There was a metallic *click*, and he fell onto his stomach as his body broke free from the dead flesh, his prosthetic a sacrifice for his freedom.

Unable to stand, he crawled across the ground—over and around bodies and through clumping pools of blood that steamed in the heat. One of the Tharkar dug their dagger into Aezik's left arm and dragged it down to his wrist. Aezik returned the favor with a well-timed swing of his war hammer, crushing her head.

There were only four now. But how much more could Aezik take?

Riddin inched forward. Peacekeeper was just beyond his reach now. He could see the gash in its frame, cut deep into the metal and stained red with blood. Blue lightning still sparked as though bleeding from a festering wound.

A wound that, as Riddin reached out to grab his gun, was

bandaged by Anezendir's hand.

His brother snatched the gun from the ground and turned its barrel on Riddin. "We could have been brothers again. You took that from us."

"Anez, don't!" he yelled. Behind him came an inhuman roar, but whether it was in rage or sorrow, he couldn't tell. He focused again on Anezendir. "We can still be brothers! Let me become king. Let me bring us peace!"

"Mordkin doesn't *deserve* peace, Riddin." Anezendir's finger curled around Peacekeeper's trigger. "You cannot give this city what it does not want. Even if you could, you wouldn't have the power to enforce it. And as I said...power isn't inherited. It's taken. Like this."

Anezendir pulled the trigger.

The half second whir as Peacekeeper charged was Riddin's death knell, but he refused to let fear overcome him. In his final moments, Riddin chose to stare into those rage-filled eyes of the dwarf he had once called his brother. The Anezendir who had grown up with him, had taught and inspired him, was dead. All that was left was the rage—the same rage that spilled through Mordkin's streets as the Khad hunted Anezendir and his Tharkar. The same rage that would, now that the gun's whirring had reached its crescendo, claim Riddin's life.

Except the whirring continued.

Anezendir's face broke into a grimace as his muscles seized around the trigger. Blue lightning lanced from the gouge in

Peacekeeper's frame. The sparks slipped between Anezendir's fingers and into his skin. The gun's low thrum grew exponentially, scaling octaves until it was a high-pitched screech.

Triumph turned into fear in Anezendir's frozen, seizing gaze.

Riddin's mind battled his own fear as it tried to problem solve by instinct. The spin coil could have been severed—he was going to die—or the elektrum core could be stuck in a recursion loop—he was going to *die*—or there could be a problem with—

Aezik's hulking form stepped over Riddin as he swung his war hammer through the air. It was a good swing. One that would have disarmed any other attacker if they had been holding any other weapon.

But this was Peacekeeper.

And Peacekeeper was broken.

In an instant that lasted an eternity, Aezik's war hammer collided with Anezendir's hand, and the whirring gun shattered. Streaks of blue lightning spiderwebbed across the swaying plains in jagged, deadly fingers as Peacekeeper exploded. They consumed Anezendir's arm, they burned Aezik's flesh, and as they touched Riddin, freezing pain lanced through him and seized every muscle in his body.

A shockwave hurled him away from the explosion's epicenter with a flash and a stone-splitting *crack*.

Pain consumed Riddin's entire consciousness. Not the pain of his body slamming back down onto the sand. Or the pain of sliding across it, his skin and clothes scraping away in the grit. No, instead, it was the internal pain of his chest. His heart pumped arrhythmically like a thick, uncoordinated lead weight. His lungs burned as they refused to fill, and his gut swarmed and stabbed his seizing muscles. Riddin was no stranger to pain, but this...All he could do was lie in his agony—still alive but wishing he had been killed.

The plains trembled as the stones beneath the sand cracked. Unbearable, blistering heat joined the far-off pain of Riddin's external body, and with an effort that felt like lifting tungsten, he dropped his head to the side and forced his eyes open.

Sand slipped between the growing cracks, draining into an unseen basin where Peacekeeper had exploded. Anezendir's body—armless, lifeless—was carried by the sands and taken down into the earth.

For a moment, the rumbling subsided as though it was satisfied. As though the mountain had accepted Aneznedir's body as a sacrifice and would spare the rest of them.

Then magma burst from the ground in a violent geyser of red-tinged liquid fire. Heat swarmed the air. Sand and stone ignited in the rapidly encroaching line of molten rock. The bodies of the dead Tharkar were consumed by the growing pool of magma.

Another geyser erupted from farther in the plains. And another. And another.

Then Riddin was flying. Weightless. Lifted from the

ground by arms he could barely feel and rushed away from the burning idea of peace behind him.

He had shattered the swaying plains, and the lake of sand was now a lake of fire.

* * *

RIDDIN'S CONSCIOUSNESS FOUGHT a losing battle against his pain as Aezik carried him through the chaos. He was loosely aware of leaving the swaying plains; of the growing pool of magma that consumed the lowest of the Unnamed buildings; of the acrid, plasmatic smell of Aezik's lightning-burnt flesh; and of Aezik's war hammer pressing against his back.

And he was aware of the screams. The cries of assaults and riots as Tharkar rose against Khad throughout slantward Mordkin. And the explosions—the well-timed, triggered explosions—that shook the city.

The high ceiling disappeared beneath the confining tunnels, and the sensation of flight ended as cold stone soaked into Riddin's back. Wherever Aezik had brought him, it seemed safe from the blistering heat that now plagued slantward Mordkin. Curious, he fought against the pain and cracked open his eyes.

And met the face of Death.

Death's faceted amber lenses reflected Riddin's agony in the dim light, while the rest of his face was covered by long gray hair and a cinched mask that gave his hollow breathing ominous air.

"You...you can't have me." Riddin's words—each a struggle between gasping breaths—were muffled to his own ears. As though he was underwater. "You...you can't..."

Ignoring his pleas, Death ripped Riddin's tunic open, exposing his sweat-soaked chest before pressing weights like anvils over Riddin's heart. They crushed the meager air from his lungs. He could feel Death reach inside his torso and pull out his heart—his soul.

"No..."

The familiar pain of lightning slammed through Riddin's body and across his heart. His muscles seized, his back arched, and his head cracked against the stone beneath him. Then he crashed back down to the ground, the jolt over in less than a second. He basked in the blissful numbness before his body recalled his pain.

Except when it returned, the thick ache of his chest was subsiding. Death's strike had melted the lead of his heart and returned it to a natural rhythm that eased his breathing and calmed his nerves. Blood and fatigue flowed free, and clarity washed through his mind.

He was in Orin's workshop. In the tunnels. The table in the corner was occupied—filled with tools and prototypes—so Aezik had laid him on the ground in the room's center. The tungsten forge to his right radiated its low light and constant heat as Orin stooped over him.

The old human plucked and prodded Riddin with

tweezers, removing splinters of metal shrapnel from his flesh. The small cutting pain barely registered in Riddin's tired mind. It felt so inconsequential.

"Easy, boy," Orin said. He raised his head, nodding to the ceiling. "Sounds like your plan went to fuck, eh?"

Riddin's head dropped back to the ground. Instead of finding pain, however, he found Aezik's gentle hand, cradling him and keeping him from slamming against the stone again. The giant dwarf gave him a hesitant smile and a solemn nod.

"How bad is it?" Riddin asked. His voice was a weak croak.

Orin shrugged as he continued his work. "Worse than before." He nodded toward the speaker, the blasted audio coming through in ringing, muffled static as the earth shook. "From what I can hear, the Unnamed are coming out of their holes. Fighting back. Those explosions have been going off across the city for about twenty minutes. Blasting powder, if I had to guess."

Riddin recalled the Tharkar war table. The points of interest marked throughout the city. They had been planning this for a long time, and now that their king was dead, they weren't going to waste any more of it. They knew where to strike.

"Now, I can tell your plan for peace didn't exactly *work out*," Orin said, "but what happened? You're gone a few minutes, and everything goes to damn. Anezendir try to kill you?"

"He...he didn't want to listen." Riddin flinched as Orin moved to bandage the severed fingers on his right hand. Amid the pain and the shock, he had forgotten losing them. "I tried, Orin. But Anez..." Anezendir's final words rattled in his mind. "Anez never wanted peace. Or maybe he did, but he felt he had to take it for himself rather than have me give it to him. I offered peace, recognition, and unity...but the Tharkar only wanted power."

"So, you killed him," Orin said. "A true dwarven show of force."

Anger chased away Riddin's fatigue. He pushed against Orin as he sat up, and one of the two anvil weights on his chest—a small elektrum gem—lanced tickling sparks across his skin. He plucked it off, its adhesive peeling away, and cast it aside.

"Anezendir killed himself." Riddin bit the words as they escaped him. "He refused my offer, set his Tharkar on me like dogs, and then tried to kill me with my own gun."

If Orin was offended by his rage, he didn't show it. "And how did you survive?"

He threw up his hand, the bandages covering his missing fingers already bloodstained. "Peacekeeper was damaged in the fight. Anez took it, pulled the trigger, and the elektrum coil fell into some sort of recursion loop. When it couldn't hold back anymore, it exploded in his face and broke the swaying plains. If it hadn't been for Aezik..."

Embarrassment consumed his anger as he realized he hadn't had a second thought for the giant who had saved his life. He twisted around to find Aezik sitting on the ground with his legs crossed and his war hammer across his lap. His posture was straight and strong, and he smiled when Riddin met his eyes, but the longer Riddin stared, the more he understood the truth.

Jagged red scars laced Aezik's skin like lightning, along with a web of bloody lines where Tharkar blades had slashed and splotchy bruises where their hammers had struck. The long gash that traveled from his left bicep down to his wrist steadily dripped blood onto the floor, and his left hand refused to fully grasp his war hammer's helve. His clothes were scorched and ashen, their swirling pattern unrecognizable. His breathing was regular, but his chest silently heaved with each breath.

But more than anything else, Riddin knew just how exhausted and hurt Aezik was by one simple fact: the giant never sat in his presence. Not when there were others in the room.

Orin moved away from Riddin—his wounds now stitched and dressed with bandages—and set to work on Aezik's injuries. "The plains breaking explains the magma filling my lower tunnels. It's undoubtedly adding to the Unnamed's desperation—losing your home will do that to you.

"So," he continued, "you killed their king, and they blame you—or Khad as a whole, more likely. And now they're seeking bloodshed, and by the sound of it, it doesn't much matter whether they're giving or receiving. At least for the moment."

"It's war," Riddin said.

"No, it's not. You'll know war when you damning see it." He lathered Aezik's cuts in a kind of lotion before wrapping them with bandages. "Before I came down here, I saw three wars.

Firsthand. And those shitting lords and ladies were getting ready for a fourth. You learn what war is real quick. It's organized. It's a red-tinged art of strategy and death, and no matter what compromises are made or what treaties are struck, it's either won or lost. This?" He waved a hand just as another explosion shook the tunnels and sent a muffled boom through the speakers in the ceiling. "This is just violence. Chaotic, uncontrolled violence. And *that* can be quelled."

"So, what can I do?" Riddin asked.

The old man glanced at Riddin, his covered face and amber eyes an unreadable mask.

"How do I stop this, Orin?"

"From my experience..." He returned to dressing Aezik's wounds. "Well, there are two ways to bring order to chaos. The first—the easiest—is to let the violence run its course. It burns hot, but it can burn quickly. Eventually, the Tharkar will either grow tired or kill each other in their foolishness. Admittedly, there isn't much of a city left standing at the end of that road, but if you keep your head down—"

"I won't let Mordkin die because of me."

"I know that, boy!" Orin took a deep breath, seeming to reign in his emotions before continuing. "I know. It's the easiest path because it requires you to do nothing, and if I know one shitting thing, it's that *you* can't do nothing. Besides, that option is for cowards anyway. For those of us who would rather bury themselves in the ground than face a fourth war. It isn't exactly the choice of a prince."

A prince.

Anezendir's words echoed through Riddin's mind: Mordkin could have no prince. Power cannot be given, only taken. Riddin's succession was a lie.

Riddin didn't believe that. He couldn't. He would prove the power of a prince.

He would save this city.

The last of Riddin's fatigue burned away in the steady heat. With an effort that strained the bandages across his body, he pulled himself to the steps at the edge of the pit. He used his hands to climb them and then sat, sweating and panting on the top step, before pushing himself up and onto his leg. It had been a long time since he'd needed to walk with only one leg, but it wasn't something easily forgotten.

Though his muscles ached and cried at the movements his mind recalled with ease, he managed to cross the room to Orin's disorganized wall of tools and scraps. "You said there were two ways to end the fighting," he said as he searched the wall. "What's the second?"

Orin watched him, the old human's deft hands mindlessly working away at Aezik's extensive wounds while he gave a careful, measured response. "You answer violence with violence. Quick, decisive violence."

Riddin looked back at him. "I'm not going to—"

"You tried with Anezendir, boy. I believe that. But now?

This rage that's spilling into Mordkin has been threatening the confines of its box for decades. I know it, and I live in a shitting hole in the ground. Listen to me when I say the only way this violence is going back *inside* its box is if it's shoved through the same hole it's spewing out of.

"The Tharkar are disorganized, leaderless—you've seen to that. You can be fuck sure any unity they have is crumbling right now. Frustration and anger is the only thing holding them together, and if you kill those feeding off it, you'll break their morale. They'll disperse. I've seen it happen again and again."

Riddin swept a row of tools aside, sending them clattering to the ground. "Those who threaten the peace are the entirety of the Unnamed! One hundred *thousand* dwarves—and you want me to slaughter all of them? *That's* your second path?"

"Have you not been listening to a shitting thing I've said? The Unnamed aren't the problem; it's the Tharkar. Kill enough of them, and their morale will break. Once that happens, the rest of the Unnamed will falter." Orin sighed and lowered his voice. He stood, now finished with dressing Aezik's wounds, and walked up to the wall next to him. "I get it, Riddin. You've spent your whole life fighting against the violence that consumes this city—the same violence that threatened you for what you are. You've been searching for a better path, and maybe—*maybe*—one exists. But not here. Not now. If you want to save this city, you need to start speaking its language."

Orin thrust his hand into the wall of tools and yanked out

exactly what Riddin had been searching for: a long rusting piece of tarnished steel that ended in a flat welded metal plate. The old man held it out for him to take.

Riddin wanted so desperately for Orin to be wrong—for there to be another option that would lead to a better outcome—but his body still ached with the consequences of trying to find another path. However, more than the struggle of indecision, he hated how similar Orin's words were to Anezendir's. That power must be taken, names must be earned, and violence must be fought with violence.

But the streets above Riddin still screamed with the echoes of his failure. His desire for a peaceful resolution was now costing countless dwarves their lives.

Maybe when Mordkin's tenuous peace was restored, he could try for a better path. But until then, he had to do what Orin said. He had to speak the city's language.

He had to fight.

Riddin snatched the metal rod from Orin's grasp. He put the welded plate on the ground and slid the old prosthetic into his waiting hip socket with a *click*. It was a crude shaft of metal, and it required him to take quick, swinging steps as he navigated to Orin's workbench. It made his unaccustomed muscles groan, but he could finally walk again.

On the workbench, the new gun prototype Orin had been working on lay uncovered, its hilt internals open for inspection. It seemed Orin had done exactly what he had set out to do: compact the components, increase the efficiency, and streamline the entire weapon. The only missing piece was the elektrum.

Riddin reached to the side of his chest and plucked the other elektrum weight off his body, its adhesive pulling at his skin. The stone that had shocked his heart back into rhythm now tickled his skin with blue lancing sparks. He pressed the gem into the waiting slot inside the grip, and the gun's internals jittered to life as power flooded through the system. Unlike Peacekeeper, this gun seemed to stay primed with energy. There would be no half second delay. Once the trigger was pulled, it would fire.

Riddin grabbed the other half of the gun's outer casing and fit it into place and set about screwing it back together. Orin had truly outdone himself. Even the frame was made of a strong thin steel compared to Peacekeeper's aluminum shell.

Except...it wasn't steel.

"Is this disiplate?" Riddin asked.

Riddin couldn't see Orin's face beneath his rebreather mask, but he could hear the smile in the old man's words. "Like that, eh? Took some doing, and there's a Prazed somewhere who's not too happy about their missing armor, but it's how I found a solution to our priming problem. It took some time though. Disiplate's hard to form. Doesn't take heat well—which is the whole shitting point, I suppose—but the result is strong. And it erases any risk of accidental electrocution." Orin tilted his head to the side. "As long as you don't damning break it."

Riddin finished securing the gun's frame while Orin

continued talking about disiplate and his desire to eventually work with Durza's ignium. And, despite Riddin's resolve to do whatever violence was necessary to save his city, an idea formed in his mind. A dangerous, hopeful idea.

A third option.

Well, a modified second option.

"Orin, how long were Aezik and I gone?" he asked.

"Well, I didn't think to count the damning seconds," Orin said. "An hour. Maybe more?"

Good. There was still time.

"You're right, Orin," he said. "I need to break the Tharkar's morale. After that, the Unnamed's resolve will dwindle. But the Tharkar aren't just Khad's problem. They pose a threat to *every* family under the mountain."

"Riddin..."

"The Tri-street conclave is happening on the bronze." He slid the gun into the sheath at his hip and walked toward Aezik, his awkward prosthetic slowing him down. "If we hurry, we can catch all the monarchs at once and convince them—Durza, Prazed, *and* my father—to join together against the Tharkar. If we can unite the families, we can break the Tharkar's morale all the sooner."

This could be it. This could be how Riddin united Mordkin.

Not in spite of violence, but *through* it.

"Alliances aren't made that easily," Orin said.

Riddin offered a hand to Aezik—not that he could have helped much—but Aezik shifted to his knee and stood on his own accord.

"Kings crave power, Riddin. Even more so in this shitting city. You saw as much with Anezendir!"

"Anez wanted to obtain power," Riddin said, pushing toward the door. "And the only way for the Tharkar to do that is to take it from the monarchs, but the monarchs want to *keep* their power. Joining together and stopping the Tharkar is in every family's best interest. I just have to make them see that."

"Words and promises won't be enough, boy."

Above, explosions shook the city, and muffled yells blasted through the workshop's speakers.

Riddin looked back at Orin as he and Aezik stood in one of the workshop's many doorways. "Then I'll find a way to make it enough."

Riddin only caught his mentor's tired, hesitant nod by the change in the reflected firelight in his amber lenses. Fighting his fatigue, he forced a smile and returned a nod of his own. Then with Aezik in tow, he limped back into the tunnels.

Toward Tri-street.

* * *

THE FARTHER THEY traveled from Orin's workshop, the more confident Riddin became in his plan.

Anezendir hadn't listened, but Anezendir hadn't wanted peace. Unnamed, ridiculed, and left to fend for himself in Mordkin's violent streets, Riddin's brother had started to see only one path forward. There was nothing Riddin could have said to sway him, he saw that now.

But the monarchs were different. They were established leaders with power and people they wanted to protect in equal measure. And Riddin's proposal was in exchange for something they would do anyway: defend themselves from the Tharkar. With the three families united under one cause—even a temporary one—it could be the first step toward the peace he wanted so badly.

All he had to do was convince three monarchs to put aside the enmity they had fostered for two hundred years.

It wasn't long before Riddin needed to stop and lean against the tunnel walls to catch his breath. His prosthetic wore on his body with each awkward step, forcing him to put more and more weight on his hip. What started as a slight chronic discomfort had quickly turned into a hitching pain that encroached on the nerves of his spine.

But he had to keep moving. He had to get to Tri-street before the conclave was over.

Despite his pain, he pushed himself away from the wall and continued walking. He only made it a hundred steps before needing to stop again. His breathing was ragged, and the sweat of effort and pain dripped off his face.

But he had to keep going. He had to reach Tri-street. He had to save this city.

The third time Riddin stopped, he nearly collapsed. Aezik pressed a firm hand down onto his shoulder, ushering him to sit. To rest.

"I can't..." Riddin said, panting. "If I stop to rest...I won't get back up... The monarchs... Who knows how long they'll be there..."

Aezik—himself breathing heavy—hesitated before giving Riddin a determined nod and moving his hand off his shoulder. The giant placed the head of his war hammer onto the ground next to Riddin and looked back and forth between the two, as if comparing him to it.

Then with surprising speed, Aezik kicked his foot down onto the war hammer's neck—down next to the head—and pried the helve with his one good arm. A sharp snap exploded through the tunnels as the metal shaft broke beneath the giant's strength. He slammed the headless shaft jagged-end down and compared it once again to Riddin before giving a satisfied nod and thrusting it into Riddin's hand in a motion that made it clear Riddin didn't have a choice in accepting it or not.

The metal rod was heavier than Riddin expected. Well-worn with a leather-wrapped handle that twisted from the top until just over halfway down. It was almost as tall as him—less a cane and more a staff—but it was far better than leaning against a wall. He took several cautious steps, and while it didn't take away the pain that had built in his hip, Aezik's gift did start to alleviate it. It would still be an effort to get to Tri-street, but this way, it wouldn't be so impossible.

Riddin looked back at Aezik. The giant studied the hammer head in his hand as though inspecting a stone ingot. He then unwrapped some of the bandaging on his left arm, lashed the head to his left hand—the one that refused to close on its own—and took several experimental swings. The hammer-fist whistled through the air, and he gave it a firm nod before he turned to meet Riddin's eyes, then glanced questioningly at the new staff.

"It's perfect," Riddin said. "I don't deserve you, Aezik. Thank you."

Aezik placed a firm hand between Riddin's shoulder blades, pushing Riddin's attention away from him and forward once again. But Riddin still caught Aezik's broad, bearded face split into a satisfied grin before they continued.

When they emerged from the tunnels in an alley next to Yaro's Bar—the front still broken and open to the city—the violence was palpable. While Riddin suspected the ground was still littered with glass, stone, and the remnants of pooled blood from that morning, it was impossible to see beneath the hundreds of churning Khad who now fought with one another, their panicked anger boiling within the city's rising heat. Thick hot smoke from the magma fumes and burning stone filled the mountain like a fog, obscuring the ceiling beneath a red-tinged cloud. Even with their filtering lungs, many gathered dwarves—Riddin included—released sputtering coughs into the sulfurous air.

Khad weren't the only ones on Tri-street though. While still confined to their own borders, the families of Durza and Prazed had also abandoned the klaxon call to clear the streets. Whether it was in answer to Khad's initial return to the streets or of their own accord, Riddin couldn't tell, but for the first time, the conclave would be held surrounded by the dwarves the monarchs led.

Arguments turned into yells, which turned into brawls. While Riddin didn't see any Unnamed or Tharkar on the street, it seemed as though every side of Mordkin had enough undirected rage that it didn't matter.

The dwarves needed someone to fight. Even if that someone was within their own ranks.

It was Aezik who kept Riddin safe while they pushed through the street. A warm tickle rose in his heart, and adrenaline stole some of the pain in his hip. He tried taking deep calming breaths and looked up at Mordkin's ceiling to find the stars, but the crimson cloud of the burning city blotted them from view.

Instead, he tried in vain to shut his ears to the clamor.

With Aezik's help, he pushed through the infighting Khad and toward the bronze plate in the middle of the street. As he neared, the distinct shouts of monarchs rose above the general clamor, though there were only two: Avash Durza and Undol

Prazed.

And like the rest of Mordkin, they were at each other's throats.

"You're weak!" Avash shouted. Her jowls vibrated with rage as her deep wrinkles emphasized a permanent animalistic sneer. "You allow the Unnamed to ravage your kingdom even as we speak!"

"You hillward cunt!" Spit exploded from Undol's lips. "My people are forced to keep the magma at bay. We fight the Unnamed as well as the very earth, and you call *me* weak? I'm tempted to let the magma consume my land just so it can rise and take *your* throne next!"

"Is that a threat?" She stepped up to Undol, her toe touching the border carved into the bronze. She raised her sword, and the blade burst into flames, powered by the orange ignium folded throughout the steel. "You would let the molten earth try to fight Durza when Prazed *clearly* cannot?"

Undol matched Avash's step and let the ignited blade rest on her disiplate cuirass, where it swallowed the flame. "I will *show* you how Prazed fights, bitch!"

"Enough!" Riddin broke free from the crowd and stepped toward the bronze.

Both Avash and Undol took a quick glance at him, then looked down at his leg. Undol turned her head away in dismissive disgust.

Avash chose to spit her disdain at his feet. "Roan

abandons the conclave—"

"—and sends his *krevtish* instead," Undol finished.

Aezik shifted at the word, his face twitching into a sneer. But he knew better than to strike another dwarf across the borders. Especially if that dwarf was a monarch.

So, Riddin's father was late too? Why? Had he been delayed by the Tharkar and the chaos in the city? Riddin had hoped to speak with all of the monarchs at once, but if he waited for his father to arrive, Avash and Undol would kill each other before he could convince them to unite.

So, with as much confidence and resolve as he could muster, he took a deep breath and stepped further onto the bronze. Taking the place meant for Khad's king.

"My name is Riddin—"

"I should kill you now," Undol told Avash, ignoring him. "My soldiers will paint Mordkin with Durza blood."

"Not before your throne burns!" Avash yelled, raising her flaming sword once again.

"I said *enough*!" Riddin slammed his staff down onto the bronze, eliciting a loud shrill ring as the sharp, sturdy metal gouged into his father's portrait. "My name is Riddin Khad. I am heir to my father's throne, and I have a proposal for you."

"A proposal, it says," Avash said.

Undol scoffed. "Khad truly has fallen if Roan sent this *thing* to beg. Killing it here would be a mercy."

"Preferable even."

Krest below, at least Anezendir had *wanted* to talk.

"You will not kill me," Riddin said. "Not before I extend my offer."

"This is useless," Avash said. "I don't have time for words—not while the Unnamed run rampant through my streets."

"The Unnamed rally behind those who have claimed the name Tharkar. *They* are the ones wanting to fight, the ones blowing up our streets. The Unnamed are simply taking advantage of the chaos. You can waste your time fighting all *one hundred thousand* Unnamed—which you *might* be able to do—or you can help me defeat what's left of the Tharkar and break the fighting at its core before either of your kingdoms fall."

"I will not be lectured by a *krevtish*," Undol snapped. "I have more than useless Unnamed to contend with. Magma rises in my streets—"

"And mine," Riddin said. "Khad reaches from hillward top to slantward bottom, in case you've forgotten." He thought back to the trickle above the throne room, the water filtering into their basin. "Khad's aquifers are full. Help me, and I will douse Prazed's side as well as Khad's. Keep the magma from consuming anything more."

The two monarchs shared a look, their rage diminishing. In that encroaching calm, he recognized desperation in their turned-away expressions. The same desperation he saw in the Unnamed when he walked through Khad's streets, on his father when he had called for Anezendir's head, and on Anezendir himself when he called for war on the swaying plains, but he could not place what it meant. What would bring all of these people together? What did they all share?

"These Tharkar," Avash hesitantly said, "who leads them?"

"No one," Riddin said. "Their king and leaders are dead already. Those who remain are passionate, angry, and unified—"

"So are the Unnamed," Undol said.

"—but we can break that unity. The Unnamed rally behind the Tharkar. We break the Tharkar, and the Unnamed will follow."

If Orin's theory was correct.

"I have no need for Khad's aquifers," Avash said. "I can handle the Unnamed—Tharkar or otherwise—without Khad's or Prazed's help."

"So can we!" Undol shouted. "Prazed can chill the magma ourselves. After that, the Unnamed will be like ants beneath our boots!"

"It sounds to me like Khad needs *our* help." Avash laughed. "If Roan Khad can't even leave his Rock to meet us, maybe he's too weak to handle a few Unnamed."

"And so he sends his *krevtish*," Undol joined. "Or perhaps it comes on its own. Perhaps Roan Khad is already dead, and it's playing king."

Riddin lifted his head to the ceiling. Every muscle in his

body tensed as he let his rage consume him. Not rage from being insulted or ignored—he had experienced that his entire life—but the rage that came with knowing his city was being devoured by violence, and he was somehow the only dwarf who cared.

Above him, fumes and smoke billowed across the ceiling. Reds and yellows that blotted out the stars with a canopy of clouds that reflected the city's rage. He knew the quartz stars were still there, but he couldn't *see* them. He couldn't *see* the hope they offered. He couldn't see their peace.

Without a release, his rage churned through him unimpeded, and evolved into panic. Anxiety. The city was on fire, drowning in molten rock and dwarven violence. He had thought Avash and Undol would see sense—that unlike Anezendir, they would care for their city as much as he did—but in the end, they were exactly like his brother. All they cared about was power: maintaining it, increasing it, and lording it over others. The power that made them so valuable—the reason Riddin needed them—was the same reason they would never listen to him.

Riddin's hand fell to his hip, his grip finding the gun there.

But also something more.

An idea occurred to him. Avash and Undol would never give up their power, even if it ensured their survival. Like Anezendir, they would rather fight and die alone and weak than fight and live united—but Anezendir *had* been willing to unite for one thing. For an increase in his power.

And while the other monarchs might never give up their power, Riddin could.

"—you Prazed bitch!" Avash snapped, her voice returning him to awareness.

"Better a bitch than a coward!" Undol yelled.

"I offer you both elektrum."

He spoke the words calmly. Almost under his breath. But elektrum, like ignium or disiplate, was a word that had a way of being heard no matter how softly it was spoken.

For the first time, both Avash and Undol looked at him, that same cursed desperation for power alight in their eyes. The same desperation that lived in the eyes of every dwarf he'd ever known. They were finally listening.

"Join my family in stopping the Tharkar," Riddin said, "and I will give you elektrum."

"Who are you to make such a promise?" Avash asked, but her resolve had already faltered to her greed.

"You know who I am." Empowered by the sway of attention, he was reminded of the Old Words and spoken contracts. "I am Riddin Khad, Roan Khad's heir, and I make this offer to you, both Avash Durza and Undol Prazed. An equal share of elektrum, to use as you wish, in exchange for your help quelling the violence that plagues our city. What say y—"

Aezik's hand yanked Riddin backward by his collar. The force choked him as a trail of blue lightning sliced an arc around the bronze plate—right through where his neck had been.

Avash and Undol stood motionless and staring ahead. They were frozen in place, save for the blood that slipped from the thin slits that appeared across their throats. Droplets that turned into unyielding floods that drenched both of their fronts in crimson.

Neither screamed or cried out or moved. Not motionless or frozen but paralyzed. Seizing. Every muscle in their bodies locked into place by the electricity coursing through them as they died standing.

Between them, on the bronze with her feet breaking the borderlines in a half crouch, was Vira. The daggers in her hands crackled with their elektrum-powered blades as she raised them level with her eyes. Eyes that looked straight at Riddin above a sickening smile.

She lunged forward, her daggers streaking through the air as she sliced at Riddin once again. By instinct—by stupid, ineffectual instinct—he closed his eyes and raised his arms in front of his face. A choice that would leave him alive and seizing once her blades made contact.

A sharp screech scraped through the air as electrified metal met stone, and the blow he anticipated never came. He opened his eyes to find Vira in that same poised half crouch, having retreated between the upright dead monarchs after another thwarted attack. Only this time, she wasn't looking at Riddin. She was looking at his monstrous defender.

Aezik stood—bent, bruised, and heaving. Blood soaked

thick streaks through the bandages around his chest while it dripped freely from his arm, those bandages now lashing his war hammer's head to his fist. He raised his arms, as though ready to fight, and the long gouge in the stone showed where he had deflected Vira's attack.

"Out of my way, you giant fuck," she said. "No one's keeping me from my birthright anymore. Not you. And not that *thing*!"

"Vira, you..." Riddin's mind fought through the too-quick events he couldn't quite track. "What are you doing? Do you realize what you've just done?"

"I've done exactly what the king sent me here to do, *krevtish*." Her daggers traced blue lines like ribbons around her. "Almost. There's still one more dwarf who needs to die today. One who should have died sixty-three years ago."

The electricity coursing through their bodies now ran its course, Avash and Undol collapsed dead to the ground. Anguished cries pierced the street from all sides, drowned out by the clashing weapons and dying screams of battle. Rage overflowed the streets, and for the first time in two hundred years, borderlines between the families were broken.

And, as if signaled to begin, Vira lunged forward once again.

Aezik threw out his hammer-fist. It swept over her as she slipped beneath his arm like a breeze. Blue streaks flashed in front of Riddin's eyes and instinct sent him stumbling backward out of reach.

She struck again, and he raised his makeshift staff like a sword to catch it. Lightning arced down the metal shaft and set the leather wrapping beneath his hand on fire as it protected him from the elektrum's effects.

A curse slipped from Vira's mouth. Seeming surprised by Riddin's defence, her next attack was slowed. Not by much but enough that he could move his staff to counter again. He shoved as they met, attempting to throw her off balance. Instead, his unyielding prosthetic betrayed him, slipping beneath his weight and sending him crashing to the ground.

The staff flew from Riddin's grip as he fell. He caught himself on the palms of his hands as a dagger passed over his head, a dodge that was a welcome surprise but one that left him exposed. Vira gave a triumphant laugh, his poor positioning a clear signal of her victory, and brought her daggers down upon him.

Aezik's hammer-fist met her descending stab before it met Riddin's flesh. The impact spun her to the side and, with a shrill *crack*, snapped one of her dagger's blades, its sharp fragments flying into the worsening chaos that surrounded them.

Screaming, Vira threw what remained of her broken blade at Aezik and dashed forward. He swatted the dagger out of the air with his hammer-fist but was left open as she jumped onto his shoulders and brought her second dagger down, aiming for the flesh at the base of his neck.

Aezik's empty right hand intercepted the dagger's path.

Electrified steel pierced his open palm and seized his fingers around her hand like a vice.

Riddin finally found his staff, and pushed off it to find his feet. His prosthetic slammed onto the stone and sent a clarifying pain vibrating up his hip and into his spine. But he regained control of his thoughts, drew his gun, and took aim at his sister.

She twisted and pulled, trying to break free from the giant who, despite his body coursing with lightning, slowly raised his hammer-fist above his head. Her face twisted in fury, and she let loose a scream that rivaled the chaos of the battle.

"This is not how I die!" she yelled.

With her free hand, Vira struck the elektrum pommel of her dagger and snapped the stone free from its hilt, sending the gem soaring out into the street. Unelectrified, Aezik's fingers slackened around her hand. She kicked away from his body and slipped her dagger free before his raised hammer-fist could sweep down and crush her skull.

Riddin tracked her movements as she sailed through the air, the barrel of his gun trained on her. When she landed in her signature half crouch, her flight finished, he didn't hesitate to pull the trigger. A condensed bullet of blue lightning shot from the barrel and straight at his sister's crouched form.

Quick as she was, not even Vira was fast enough to avoid lightning. She dodged to the right, but the condensed bolt still tore through her chest, just beneath her heart. The momentum of the blow sent her spinning backward and onto her stomach.

Riddin kept the gun trained on his sister, prepared to fire again if needed.

Impossibly, she staggered to her knees and looked down at the gory hole in her chest. With fingers Riddin had never known to be gentle, she brushed the wound in tender disbelief and pulled a blood-soaked hand away.

Then she met Riddin's eyes. Her face was painted with that familiar look of disgust she reserved just for him, amplified by her rage and shock. "You tried to *kill* me?!"

Riddin didn't have the chance to respond. From the smoke-filled battlefield that surrounded them, a spear found its terminus through the back of Vira's head, out of her open mouth, and into the stone where she knelt, pinning her to the ground.

For a single horrific moment, Vira lived—the shock on her face now the only expression left. Her bottom jaw moved, listless and silent as it ground against the spear's shaft, and her eyes lulled upward to meet Riddin's, as though searching for an answer to the unfamiliar pain she felt. Then her expression slackened, her eyes went dull, and her lifeless body settled against the spear.

Riddin couldn't move, his arm still outstretched, his gun still aimed.

Vira was...dead?

Off to the side, Aezik moved as though nothing had happened. As though he hadn't nearly died alongside her. For some reason, the giant hurried to unlash the war hammer head from his left hand, the blood-soaked bandages furling in the infernal breeze as they fell to the ground. Riddin couldn't understand it. Why release his weapon? Didn't he see what was happening?

From the choking chaos that flowed around them, a young dwarf dressed in dyed white leathers and who had yet to even grow his beard found Avash Durza's body on the bronze. He looked so much like Avash. A son? A...prince?

Five others, all dressed in Durza leathers, followed close behind. They were screaming. Bloody, murderous war cries as they looked from Avash's body to Riddin—the last living dwarf on the bronze.

And, led by the young Durza, they charged.

The head of Aezik's war hammer shot through the air, passing in front of Riddin's face, before colliding with the boy's head. It sank into crushed bone like sand and threw him backward onto the ground. The other Durza didn't break pace as they rushed over their prince's body without care or thought to who he had been.

A Durza hefted a flaming spear over her shoulder—another spear?—and took aim as she ran. She held the weapon steady despite her screaming sprint, then threw it at Riddin.

A distant part of Riddin's mind reacted. He raised the staff in his hand—when had he picked that up?—in an effort to deflect the spear even though he *knew* it was pointless. He was not his sister; his reflexes wouldn't be enough.

Her reflexes hadn't been enough.

Riddin was once again yanked to the side, and the spear's flaming blade extinguished as it sank into Aezik's left shoulder.

The giant had saved him yet again. Why?

Aezik threw Riddin back, sending him stumbling to the ground. He reached up to break the spear off at his shoulder but, as though thinking better, yanked the spear from his flesh instead. The crimson spearhead ignited as ignium met air, and the heated metal cauterized his wound as he pulled it free and took a ready stance against his opponents.

From the other side of the street, three Prazed emerged from the smoke, their ornate metal disiplate bathed with yellow in the diffused firelight. Like the Durza before them, they looked at the carnage at Riddin's feet—at Undol lying dead on the bronze—and broke into a charge of their own.

Aezik shuffled. His attention darted between the two encroaching groups as though desperately strategizing: trying to devise a battle plan that resulted in one dwarf overcoming eight.

And it was seeing that panic that finally broke Riddin from his stupor.

Riddin raised his gun and fired into the five charging Durza—the closer of the two groups. Two lightning bullets tore through flesh while a third shot wide, over a dwarf's head and into the crowded street, destined to kill someone of unknown allegiance Riddin couldn't afford to think about.

He wouldn't be distracted again. Not now.

Their charge ending, Aezik launched into the remaining Durza with strength and a flaming spear, while Riddin pivoted against his prosthetic—pain shooting up his back—to take aim against the Prazed.

His first shot didn't tear through flesh or metal. Blue lightning broke and arced across the lead Prazed's disiplate, scattering the energy into nothing but kinetics. Kinetics that, while nonlethal, slowed the Prazed's charge with the impact.

Riddin adjusted his aim and fired two, three, four shots at the lead's feet. Lightning dissipated, but the shock of the momentum tripped the dwarf in his charge, sending him crashing to the ground and sliding across stone.

A jagged blade sliced a vibrating cut across Riddin's prosthetic, stabbing a sharp pain in his hip socket. The last of the Durza must've dodged around Aezik's defenses and attempted to hamstring him. When Riddin didn't collapse on a hindered leg, however, the dwarf looked up at him in confusion.

Riddin met the look with a bolt of lightning that tore a hole through the Durza's skull.

Riddin returned his attention to the Prazed in time to see Aezik catch the head of a descending war hammer and save him from being crushed. The giant twisted the weapon out of the Prazed's hands with a practiced grace, then spun it around in a fell swing that collided with the dwarf's back. Armor folded, and the dwarf screamed as his spine snapped between his shoulder blades.

The new war hammer twirled in Aezik's functioning

hand. It looked like a toy compared to the one he had sacrificed in the tunnels. The one that was now Riddin's staff.

The remaining two Prazed swayed and hesitated as they faced a fight that was, finally, equal.

Except it didn't stay equal for long. From the smoke, more Durza and Prazed emerged— finding their dead monarchs, filling with rage, and filing into rank. What was two Prazed became a dozen of each family ready to fight, their directionless anger making any on the bronze a target. Riddin's skin crawled with adrenaline and anxiety as both sides twisted and snarled.

But the Tharkar arrived before they could whet their bloodlust.

Blasts exploded throughout Tri-street. The ground shook, sending Riddin to his knees as dwarven bodies and parts were thrown into the air all around them from the blasting powder. The Unnamed and Tharkar suffocated the crowded street as they flooded in from every direction and added to the chaos.

Orin had said Riddin would recognize war when he saw it. Organized and violent. Was this it? Was every family fighting each other in a burning, exploding city enough to be called war?

Or was war somehow worse than this?

"We can't stay here," Riddin said. Whatever this was—war or chaos—they were in the middle of it: forced to protect themselves from all sides. And he knew no Khad would come to their aid here.

Aezik gave a determined nod, and when the tension on the

bronze broke and the fighting began, he grabbed Riddin's shoulder and pushed him hillward, through the violence, and back into Khad territory.

Battle-worn and limping, Riddin and Aezik both fought through skirmishes not unlike that first, only now with flashes of green, copper-dyed cloth alongside white leather and plate armor. Riddin's mouth became coated with the acrid taste of sulfur and the rust of blood that hung in the air. He climbed over dead dwarves of every allegiance, and his mind grappled with the fact that the mountain itself was being suffocated by the conflict all around him.

Riddin somehow managed to reach the edge of Tri-street before collapsing. Without breaking stride, Aezik dragged him by his collar and brought him to rest safely against the wall of a hillward building. The panting, exhausted giant somehow stayed upright, towering over Riddin and shielding him from the battle as he leaned against the same wall for support.

From their paused vantage, Tri-street spread out below them, Riddin watched the carnage unfold. The red and black colors of Khad crashed like waves—dwarves charging into the fray and running for their lives in equal measure. Weapons swept through the air, creating swirls in the smoke that cleared and obscured the carnage in equal measure.

Riddin watched the encroaching lines of shining disiplate metal and bleached white armor. Of Prazed and Durza with flashes of Tharkar green spread throughout their ranks. They pushed together against the black and red frontlines of his family.

Riddin would have laughed if he hadn't been so tired. Despite the death and the screams and the rising dread that sank his stomach, he couldn't help but see the irony that slaughtered his people. He had gotten exactly what he had wanted. After two hundred years, the families were finally united against a common enemy.

They were united against Khad.

Riddin finally understood Orin's words. The Tharkar had incited violence. They had risen from the city's crevices to create a disorganized chaos that had threatened Mordkin in microcosm. That could have been stymied, beaten back, and policed.

But this? This was more than family against family. This was strategy. This was front lines and battlefields. This was the sounds and tastes of death and blood.

This was war.

And it was one they were losing.

"We have to help them," Riddin said. He pulled himself up by his staff, shaking with the effort. His leg buckled, his knee bent, and he slammed back onto the ground. "I have to help them. I have to—"

Aezik yanked him up by the front of his shirt. Not to his feet but into the air. The giant flicked his gaze left to right, searching Riddin's eyes as he hung there, limply. Then he nodded as though he understood.

Of course he did. He was Aezik.

Aezik then threw Riddin into the wall he had been leaning against.

The hard rock Riddin expected to break against had vanished. Instead, he flailed through the air as the ground swallowed him. His staff fell from his grip with a clattering echo, and the light of the city retreated from the darkness of the tunnels.

When he finally landed, Riddin's head cracked back against the ground. His vision flashed white, stealing his other senses and replacing them with pain. The sounds of the battle just outside the tunnel were muffled and far, and his head lulled with a daze that made him feel both light and heavy.

When he finally managed to regain his sight and prop himself up onto his elbows, the light from the tunnel's entrance was fading with the grinding sound of stone as Aezik shut Riddin inside.

"Aezik!" Riddin's words were thick and tired. In his disorientation, he clawed up the wall to get back onto his feet. "Aezik, what are you doing? I have to help!"

Aezik held out a halting hand, and despite himself, Riddin paused his approach. He stared ahead: at the shrinking gap of light, at Aezik's battle-weary face.

The giant dwarf's left arm hung limp—gray, blood soaked, and useless at his side. Cuts, bruises, and burns traced bloody spiderwebs across his body, staining his torn clothes and bandages. They were only there because Aezik had saved Riddin from the Tharkar, from Vira, and from Prazed and Durza. What had

Riddin ever done to deserve the giant's devotion, his sacrifices?

Aezik pointed at Riddin, then past him—farther into the tunnels; hillward. Then he placed his right hand over his chest and nodded.

No... Not a nod. A bow. A farewell.

And Riddin understood just how much more Aezik was willing to sacrifice for him.

Riddin stumbled forward. "Aezik."

The tunnel grew dark again as the giant reached to the side with his good arm and resumed closing the stone door over it.

"Aezik, please don't! I need yo—"

It was Riddin's good leg that betrayed him. In the dark, his foot found his staff. It rolled out from beneath him and threw him forward onto the rough stone, sending pain vibrating through his prosthetic and into his hip.

He caught a final glimpse of Aezik's face—smiling in the fading light—as the giant shut him away from the war: saving Riddin's life by sacrificing his own. Unable to do anything else, Riddin reached out a desperate hand.

And he was plunged into darkness before he could beg his friend to stay.

* * *

DWARVES WERE MADE to be lost. Their eyes could adjust to see in the pitch black. Their lungs could filter anything, be it particulate or toxin. Their skin could endure abuse as well as any stone. More than anything, they faced a hesitant, unsure life with certainty. When the world grew dark, suffocating, and serrated, dwarves were the ones who survived. Thrived.

And here, lost in the dark and unable to see a path forward, Riddin realized the truth.

He wasn't a real dwarf.

A real dwarf would be fighting in the streets, not hiding in the tunnels. A real dwarf would have laughed at the idea of establishing peace on the bronze amid the chaos. A real dwarf would have gone to Anezendir for his head, just like Riddin's father had ordered.

A real dwarf wouldn't have been born a *krevtish*.

Maybe Vira was right. Maybe he deserved to die at birth, and Roan had made a mistake in sparing his life. Perhaps if his father had done so, none of this would have happened. Without him, Mordkin might still be at peace. Anezendir, Vira, the monarchs...and Aezik—they would all still be alive if he had just done the right thing and died the moment he had left his mother's womb. Or had spared her life, too, and died before then.

But he hadn't. And they weren't.

Using the walls as his support, Riddin crawled back onto his feet before bending down to pick up his staff. He gingerly shifted his weight onto his prosthetic, and his flesh yielded to the metal with a slow-stabbing pain. He didn't know where he was going. His body simply needed to move.

The walls echoed with the clack of Riddin's staff and the muffled screams from the streets above. He couldn't leave from the entrance Aezik had sealed, which meant his only path was farther into the tunnels. There were three other exits close by. If he wanted to rejoin the fighting, he could leave through one of those, and if he was a real dwarf, maybe that was what he would have done.

Instead, he went deeper. Hillward. In the direction Aezik had told him to go, though not where the giant had meant. Aezik had wanted him to return to Khad Rock—return to safety. But with every twist and turn through the tunnels, he recognized he wasn't going back home. Not yet.

But it wasn't until Riddin stopped outside the elektrum-powered security door that he realized where he had been going and why. He needed advice. Wisdom. From someone who had experienced war themselves. After the massacre on the bronze, there were only two people left in all of Mordkin who had that experience.

His father had seen one war. Two hundred years ago.

Orin had seen three in the past sixty.

Riddin waited for the telescopic lens to descend from the ceiling.

Whatever the old man's advice, he would take it. No fighting, no tweaking, and none of his own ideas that had only led to more pain. If Orin told him to die a martyr for his city, he would do it. If he told him to kill for it, he would. He had taken

Orin's experience for granted, even as the man had recognized and cautioned against the warning signs of war. Not anymore. Not again.

"Orin?" Riddin called to the hidden lens. His voice cracked with the desperation he was trying to suppress. "Orin, it's me. It's Riddin."

Nothing.

Riddin knew better than to touch an elektrum-powered door, but the leather-wrapped handle of his staff had protected him from Vira's daggers. As long as he didn't linger...

He gave the wooden door a quick knock with his staff. He expected the crackle of lightning and the smell of burning leather as the tip slammed against the door's metal scaffolding, but neither came. Instead, the door creaked open without resistance, leading into a dark room with a cold forge.

The workshop was far from empty, but as he searched the abandoned room, he identified the skilled hands that had scoured it before his arrival. A selection of tools were missing, scraps of metal had been pried from their shelves, and the empty elektrum sockets that had once powered so many of the strange devices he had helped design were gone. They all betrayed a simple, unavoidable fact.

Orin had fled.

Riddin shouldn't have been surprised. He shouldn't have screamed—not when he had just finished suppressing his emotions from the tunnels. He shouldn't have raged around the workshop, throwing everything Orin had left behind across the room until the floor was littered with the other abandoned refuse not even worthy of a goodbye. He shouldn't have cried when he felt the residual heat of the forge that betrayed how close he had been to catching Orin before he had left the mountain in the wake of war.

It was ridiculous to imagine Orin would have been any help in ending this conflict. The old man had admitted he'd buried himself under the ground rather than face a fourth war. He should have known a fifth would have driven him back to the world above.

But he had hoped...

No. Orin's advice would have been to run. To abandon this city. To take that first option he had offered to Riddin—the coward's path.

But Riddin couldn't do that. This was his city. It was burning and bleeding, and he knew no one else was going to save it. No one else would pull it back from the brink of destruction. That was *his* responsibility. He was heir, and although Anezendir might have been right, and the other dwarves might not think that word held any meaning, it meant something to Riddin.

It meant he couldn't run.

If only it told him what he *could* do.

Instead, he was alone, surrounded by memories in the husk of what had once been his sanctuary. The forge he had helped Orin design was now cold. The speakers in the ceiling above and the constant hum of the security systems were now silent thanks to their stolen power sources.

With a startling laugh, Riddin realized Orin would never replace his prosthetic. The old man had come to Mordkin with ideas and designs, but Riddin had given him the gift of electricity to make them real. What had Orin given him? Advice, which he had ignored. A gun, which he had destroyed...

No.

No, Peacekeeper had been his own creation. Riddin had used the old man's workshop and tools, but Peacekeeper was his design. A flawed, imperfect, destructive design prone to malfunctioning but *his*. One he had built from the skeletons of his first designs, and while it hadn't kept the peace like he had wanted, the end result—the replacement gun Orin *had* given him—had saved lives even as it had taken them. It had helped Khad flee from the encroaching families skirmish after skirmish. It might not have been a tool for peace, but it had been invaluable in war.

If only all of his designs could be used to...

An idea etched itself into Riddin's mind, and from it formed a plan. A path forward through the conflict that raged over his head, a way to save this city. It wasn't the full path, but it was a step. The first step. Enough.

It would mean death. Destruction. He could save as many dwarves as he could before his show of force, but at this point, it would be unavoidable. Like the other dwarves of Mordkin, he would have to push through his hesitancy, his uncertainty. His hands would be stained with blood—more than they already were—but if peace was waiting at the end of that road? *Real* peace?

Riddin might not be a real dwarf.

But if it meant saving Mordkin—saving his people—he could become one.

* * *

RIDDIN DISCONNECTED HIS prosthetic—the temporary reprieve barely registering to him—as he prepared for his climb. Using his makeshift staff in one hand and his prosthetic in the other, he dug into the slanted walls, pulled himself out of the underground tunnels, pushed open the trap door from below, and rolled out into his sparse room inside Khad Rock.

Exhaustion tempted him to rest, but like his pain, it was timid in the face of his desire. He snapped his leg back into his hip with a dull clink. The climb had damaged the connection, so the prosthetic shifted and twisted in its socket as he pushed himself to his feet and walked out into the halls.

Red and black patterns swirled around him as dwarves dressed in Khad clothing ran through the Rock. Some were pristine and determined, while others were battle-worn and tired. All had smiles on their faces, enjoying the violence like animals.

When Riddin pushed into the throne room, the encroaching sounds of scraping metal and painful screams told him the front line was nearly at the Rock's door already. Dwarves fled and fed that line in equal measure, their numbers ebbing and flowing out of the throne room's entrance. In the balcony above, the ancient ballistae and javelins that had been maintained these last two centuries fired mercilessly.

Riddin pushed past all of it. He cut through the flowing crowd, crossed the room, and took the first step of his slow ascent up the side staircase.

He spared a glance at the throne. Empty. His father was undoubtedly in the front lines.

So, he climbed. Above the throne room, above the balcony, above everything. Up to his familiar station at the top of the tallest, oldest building in the city and directly beneath Khad Rock's aquifer. There, he found the panel he had created to control his earliest designs from almost thirty years ago. Back when maintaining the aquifer had been Aezik and his station. Before he had been named heir.

Below, the combined might of every dwarf in Mordkin pressed against the faltering line of Khad. Flashes of ignium fire and elektrum lightning exploded through the line as Durza and Khad forces met, while the same bursts of energy evaporated into the void that was Prazed's disiplate.

Riddin expected the sounds of clanging metal, the shouts of triumph and defeat, and even the distant explosions of Tharkar blasting powder—all of which screamed throughout the city. But he hadn't anticipated how loud the sound of squelching flesh and breaking bones would be.

The distant city was obscured by the same sulfurous haze that choked Mordkin's ceiling. Painted with the yellow and red of the rising magma, the air shimmered with a roiling heat that was impossible to ignore. The waging war beneath him was a problem, but so was the magma.

Fortunately, he could solve both with the flip of three levers.

With the pull of the first lever, the klaxon alarm over the ballistae spun to life, elektrum powering the whirling chopper and spitting air through the alarm's horn in the same high-pitched whine that had cleared the streets earlier that morning. This had been Riddin's first design: wiring and tooling the once manual crank to spin with the power of electricity.

Confusion cut through the fighting and paused the ballistae, but the stutter in combat didn't last long. The Khad klaxon only sounded for two reasons. Even in the context of peace, this was an urgent call to find shelter and clear the streets.

In the context of war, it was a signal to retreat.

The siege weapons resumed their cadence, and the front line faltered as Khad heeded the alarm and returned to the Rock. In the wake of retreat, the other families pushed their advantage. His hand ready and waiting on the second lever, Riddin watched with forced indifference as the slowest Khad were cut down from behind. Once the street was cleared of swirling specks of red and black, he flipped it.

Riddin's second design had taken a bit more work. He had learned to turn electrical energy into kinetic with the alarm, but Khad Rock's massive stone doors needed far more energy to open and close. He designed a looping electromagnet Orin had called "inspiring" when he explained it to the old man years later, but the most difficult part of the design had been convincing his father for that much elektrum.

The proof of the design's success now resonated with the sound of grinding stone as the doors closed beneath him and separated his family from the rising insurmountable tide. Without the risk of killing Khad with their poor aim, the ballistae fired faster than ever, slaughtering the attackers as they were shut out of the Rock.

The screams of death turned into shouts of triumph and frustration as the united forces of Durza, Prazed, Tharkar, and Unnamed all threw themselves at Khad Rock's doors. The stone beneath Riddin's feet shook with the force of it, but beneath the rising clamor was a familiar hum. A whir.

When Riddin had been stationed up here by his father, the entire Khad family had treated it like a joke. Riddin, the *krevtish* who couldn't even stand on his own, was given a responsibility no one wanted, and that no dwarf—not even twenty dwarves—could perform alone. They had expected him to fail, and when the call for volunteers to help his station came, they had all guaranteed that failure by declining the service. All but one.

An outcast. A colossus of a dwarf.

Perhaps Roan Khad had thought the idea of Aezik helping Riddin was funny. Khad's strongest dwarf paired with its weakest, both responsible for something they would never be able to achieve, even together. Perhaps his father viewed it as a consolation for giving them such an impossible role.

But Riddin had used it as an opportunity.

The amount of elektrum necessary to power Riddin's third design would have been beyond the family stores, so he designed a way to increase the power of a single gem. The high-pitched whirring that was growing around him was the sound of electricity building up and condensing through a giant spin coil. The design had needed a special security measure, one Riddin had built into the other two levers, which also closed the circuit necessary to start building up the needed electricity. Power flowed in but had no way out.

At least not yet.

The aquifer's eight floodgates were solid, strong, heavy stone that hung over Khad Rock's walls, above channels that fell to the streets below. They had once required a team of dwarves to open, working together to crank and twist the mechanical water wheel to open the gates bit by bit. Riddin had changed that.

Riddin flipped the third switch. The building's whir ended with a crack as the condensed electricity zipped through an accelerator, split into eight directions, and shot into the awaiting gates' locking mechanisms.

What would have taken two dozen dwarves minutes took Riddin seconds as all eight floodgates burst open, releasing their water in a torrent down Khad Rock's walls and onto the streets below. In the fell cascade of hundreds of thousands of gallons, the dwarves who fought against Khad's door were swept away from the Rock, fated to either drown as they were carried slantward or to meet the boiling magma the water would eventually cool.

Dread gnawed Riddin's heart as he looked out at a city being washed away. Despite the roaring water rushing around him and the lungs of his adversaries now filling with water, he thought he could hear their screams.

Thousands of dwarves would die because of that water—because of him. Just like the thousands who had died in the magma Anezendir had released in the swaying plains. Or those caught in the explosions set off by the Tharkar throughout the city afterward. Or the countless deaths of the war started by his sister's assassination of the monarchs.

This was no different. He was no different.

But this was what was required.

As water and flesh met the magma below, and the choking volcanic fumes were chased away by the steam of death that would eventually give way to the stars he longed to see, Riddin finally understood the simple truth he had been fighting against his entire life. He understood why he had never been able to keep the peace in a city corrupt with rage. He understood the law of Mordkin.

Peace could only be established through violence.

With another pull of the first and third levers, he closed the floodgates before the aquifers were completely emptied and turned off the klaxon alarm, disrupting the aquifer's circuit. Then with a heavy, limping step, he twisted and descended back down the stairs and into the crowded throne room.

It was so quiet. No one yelled in triumph or relief. Instead, the room was filled with the low murmur of the angry and the misguided seeking a path forward and the silence of anticipation.

Riddin's cane and prosthetic broke that silence as his slow, dull, clinking steps descended into the crowd. Coming into view, he found the source of the anticipation standing in full, resplendent plate armor—with Throat Cleaver crackling in his hand.

"Riddin?" Roan asked. "*You*?"

Riddin recognized the tone of disbelief in his father's voice. It was the same disbelief he showed whenever he defied Roan's expectations. As he reached the bottom of the stairs, and the gathered Khad split between him and his father, however, he wondered why Roan held such disbelief now. Why was Roan so surprised to see him?

"I was told of your triumph over Anezendir in the plains," Roan said, an air of command returning to his words, "but I couldn't bring myself to believe it! Riddin, my son, killing the traitor himself? Ah, but now, when I look at you—at all you have done—I see the truth. I see there is no other possibility."

Roan stepped forward, surrounded by the battle-weary

crowd, and met Riddin with a gauntleted hand on his shoulder. The jolt of weight forced Riddin's prosthetic to dig into his flesh with sudden extreme pain, but he refused to flinch. After all, he was familiar with pain. It was the only companion he had left.

"Tell me," Roan said. "Where is your sister?"

"Dead." The memory of her attack. Of him shooting a hole in her chest. Of the spear exploding through her mouth. "Killed."

"By your own hand?"

He nodded.

"Fascinating." Roan's face split into a broad smile. He leaned in close, his beard scratching Riddin's ear, and his tone grew sickly sweet. "Vira thought you were weak, but I've always known your potential, Riddin. From the very beginning. It's why I saved you from death after your birth. Why I raised you to be brutal when you couldn't be strong. Why I named you my heir. You've always been the one I felt could be king."

Except Roan Khad hadn't raised him. Anezendir had. Roan hadn't taken pride in him. He had locked him away in the aquifers. And Riddin hadn't been the brutal one. That had been Vira.

So why *had* Roan named him heir?

"Now look at what you've brought us!" Roan screamed. He released Riddin and strode past him into the crowd with Throat Cleaver crackling in his hand. "My heir has broken the peace! Riddin Khad has delivered us *war*!"

The gathered dwarves yelled in triumph. They raised their weapons and shouts and allowed their rage to chase away their fatigue. Their bloodlust had been roused by so few words.

Well, Riddin could speak too.

"Peace?" Riddin asked. "Tense, threatening violence around every corner isn't peace, Father. Mordkin has *never* known peace."

"And it never will!" Roan laughed. "Don't you see the beauty of it, boy? We've done nothing but grow fat and weak these last two hundred years. *That* is what peace has done to us. We *need* war. And look at what war has brought us!" He threw a hand back toward Riddin as though offering him up to the churning, hate-filled crowd. "War has given me an heir worthy of my throne. War is a king maker!"

In the roar that followed, Roan's actions finally made sense to Riddin. His father had never established laws in Mordkin because he wanted violence. He had called for Anezendir's death, despite knowing what it would do to the Unnamed, because he wanted a revolt. He had sent Vira to the bronze to kill the monarchs while he stayed behind and donned his armor in preparation for the war he *wanted*.

And he had sent Riddin to the bronze in his place.

Riddin's father wasn't surprised he had survived the swaying plains or the war in the streets. He was surprised Riddin had killed his assassin.

A rhythmic barrage beat against the door as dwarves,

recovered from the deluge, once again laid siege to Khad Rock. It grew, betraying just how many dwarves had survived Riddin's flood, and inside the throne room, apprehension and excitement rose in the Khad dwarves who were still hungry for blood.

Roan turned away from Riddin, Throat Cleaver crackling an arc through the air as he pointed at the door. "And now the bastards have returned to claim my throne for themselves! Listen! Even now, they fight for the opportunity to die by our blades. Our power!"

A cheer rolled through the crowd, spears and swords and hammers and axes all raised into the air. Some even crackled with the same blue rage that danced along Throat Cleaver's edge.

They had lost themselves to their bloodlust.

Rage flowed through Riddin as well, building into a turmoil that tensed every muscle in his body. The gun in his hand grew heavy. His finger teased the trigger. Unlike the others, he didn't want blood. He wanted something more—he wanted it so badly he couldn't *breathe.*

But instead of giving in, Riddin looked up.

For a moment, he was back at the aquifers, the steam chasing away the toxic fumes that obscured the quartz stars. He couldn't see them here in the throne room. He hadn't been able to since all this began—trapped beneath the tunnels and the smoke and the sulfur. He had lost sight of the peace the stars offered, but through faith, he knew they were there, waiting to twinkle endlessly once the violence had finally passed. He could almost see them. The memory of them.

And with a long exhale, he gave his rage to the memory—the promise—of the stars.

The power to bring everlasting peace to Mordkin was right in front of him. Like Anezendir had said: All he had to do was take it.

"Open these doors!" Roan screamed into the tumultuous crowd. "Let us show our enemies the power of Khad! Let us greet them with lightning and death until none stand in our way. Until Khad is the only name left under the mountain!"

"No."

When Roan Khad turned to look back at his son, excitement and fury alive on his face, Riddin had already pulled the trigger. The bullet of condensed blue lightning struck him between the eyes and bore a hole through his skull. Locked by electricity, his body slammed backward onto the ground like a metal statue—an out-of-rhythm beat alongside the banging siege of war.

In the silence that followed, Riddin turned away from the crowd and took step after agonizing step until he reached the foot of the five shallow stairs that led up to the Khad throne.

And he began to climb.

"We will bring peace to this city." His voice was low, but it carried over those who had once questioned his strength. "We—"

"Fuck that!" someone yelled. "Why should we listen to a *krevtish*? We should—"

Riddin didn't recognize the dwarf as he shot them. The dwarves around them let their body fall stiff and heavy onto the stone. None of them seemed to care. They were all looking at him now—*finally* looking at him.

"We will bring peace to this city," Riddin repeated. "We will kill those we must, but when their morale is broken, we will offer them a path forward that is not death. That is my law. What say you?"

He had expected a scattered mumble of agreement. Or dissent. But instead, a sudden roar of affirmation echoed through the hall with enough force to give the banging rhythm of siege pause.

He continued his ascent in the tense, pounding silence until he reached the top of the five steps. He stood alone. Above every Khad dwarf who cowered behind the Rock's walls—behind *his* walls. And he stared down at his inheritance.

His hands were covered in filth and blood, but they were calm. They didn't tremble, even though he felt they should. They simply held his gun. The weapon he had designed as a peacekeeper in a city that had never known peace. Perhaps that was why the first one had so many problems. So many malfunctions that resulted in catastrophe.

But Riddin knew better now. He knew what this weapon really was. He'd found its true name in the destruction it dealt. In where it had put him—above the Khad family, the empty throne at his feet. This weapon was nothing but violence and war.

And war was a king maker.

Electrified metal scraped against stone on the ground behind him. He twisted around, King Maker raised and pointed at the dwarf who dared to pick up his father's sword. Who dared to challenge his rule.

And he froze.

Blood-soaked, with a haphazardly wrapped bandage around the stump of what had once been his sleeveless left arm, Aezik pried Throat Cleaver from Roan Khad's still-clenched fist, then met Riddin's eyes. He was injured—a *krevtish* now like Riddin—but he was alive. Slow and tired and soaking wet, but *alive*.

With sodden steps, Aezik moved through the crowd that parted for him and the crackling blade he held. He climbed the shallow steps to the throne—to Riddin—and stared down at him. A tension built in the room from the hearts of dwarves who didn't understand the truth, who only saw Throat Cleaver and King Maker and not those who wielded them.

At the top of the steps, Aezik turned Throat Cleaver around, then buried its tip into the stone at Riddin's feet before kneeling.

Like a crashing wave, the apprehension in the room broke, and the gathered dwarves knelt in turn—in the balconies, behind the pillars, and stuffed halfway into the Rock's hallways. They all knelt and bowed their heads.

All except Aezik, who kept his eyes locked on Riddin's.

With visible effort, the giant fought against the bruises that swelled his face and gave a broad, beard-splitting grin filled with pride. One Riddin returned without hesitation.

"M-my king?"

It took Riddin a moment to recognize the dwarf in the sling, a half hammer held tight in his good arm.

"My king," Viz said. "How're we to, uh, meet our enemies? Will we open the doors and charge out t' meet them like the k... Like your father said?"

"No," Riddin said. "That will only end in our deaths. I won't lead you into an unwinnable slaughter. If we wish to bring peace to Mordkin, we cannot die today." Orin's words came to him as a reminder. "We must win this war."

"Then...what?"

Riddin gazed out at the Khad crowd. There were thousands of them. All finally willing to listen. None willing to act without the word of their king.

So, this was power.

He glanced at Aezik in front of him. Bruised and bloody and...sopping wet. Aezik had been outside the Rock when Riddin had opened the floodgates. When the only way in had been shut.

Except there *was* another way inside. One that led throughout the entire city. One that would let Khad flank their attackers and strike them down without ever opening the Rock's doors. One that no one but him and Aezik knew existed.

All Riddin had to do was speak.

And when he did, he spoke with the voice of a king. "There are tunnels..."

THE END

Postscript

Thank you for reading *King Maker*! If you enjoyed it, please consider leaving a rating and review on your favorite platform (or two. I mean, no one's watching...). Ratings are the #1 way to support me and my work as I continue to work on bigger and better things.

And if you want to keep up to date with those bigger and better things, there's no better way than subscribing to my newsletter. I give weekly updates and short stories that are filled with exclusive deals and behind the scenes info, including a free prequel short story to *King Maker* called *Flowers for Hekii*!

Sign up here: https://quainholtey.substack.com/subscribe

Or follow this QR code:

If you're reading this postscript and wondering why the story is over, yet there's still so much book left, I'd encourage you to read my Author's Note at the beginning of the book. If that's too much of a hassle, however, then let me give you the short version.

So much changed between *King Maker*'s 9th draft (the story you just read) and its first, and I wanted to share what the original version of the story looked like as a "Special Feature."

What follows is my first draft of King Maker, completely unedited. It is the exact same story, only very, very different.

If, like me, deleted scenes and special features are something you love, then I sincerely hope you enjoy seeing where King Maker started: poor grammar, plot holes, character inconsistencies, and all.

And if not, that's okay, too.

Regardless of what you choose to do, I want to thank you again for reading *King Maker*. As hard as I work on my stories, they are never truly finished until they are read and live in someone else's mind.

I hope you enjoyed my transcribed hallucinations. I look forward to sharing more with you in the future.

With a Smile,
Quain Holtey

King Maker
The First Draft

ONE OF THE benefits of organized crime is that it can be done in broad daylight without attracting any risk or attention. Of course, Mordkin was a city built from the quarried earth and mines of a hollowed mountain, where the dwarves lived and worked and breathed the stale, precisely humid air of perpetual night beneath a canopy of rock and stone.

Gas streetlamps burned a ghostly yellow, almost green, that contrasted against the bright warm firelight shining through windows of storefronts and towering houses that made the dwarves forget about the stars they never saw. And in the peace of evening late enough to be called night, yet not too late to be called morning, a comfortable murmur of dying street conversations and drowsy vagrants rested on the city like a thin blanket growing thicker with the threat of silence.

Until the dwarf was hurled through the storefront window of Weddin's Bar. Noise of the fight inside the Bar's stone walls burst onto the street, sweeping away the night's looming silence. Soon after, three more dwarves exited Weddin's, though they had the fortune of being sent stumbling and scurrying out the establishment's front door as they were chased away by seven others who wore fine, patterned red clothes that, in the light of fire and gaslamp, painted them several shades deeper than the sun would have.

"And stay out!" one of the pursuers yelled. The others cheered and jibed as he looked back through the broken window into Weddin's. "What d'ya say, Riddin? Should we remind those Tharkar bastards their place in our city?"

Inside, Riddin accepted a bag of chilled stones from the barkeeper and rested the pouch on the knuckles of his right hand. The stones inside cascaded loosely over the already-bruising flesh, chilling every crevice with painful pleasure.

Riddin, exchanging one bag for another, gave the barkeeper a small bag of gold. "For the trouble," he told Weddin. "Gotta keep Mordkin pretty, eh? Even if we're the ones fuckin' it up." He shared a chuckle with the barkeeper as he stepped through the broken window.

"We ain't responsible for this!" one of the others said. He placed a heavy boot on the chest of the man Riddin had thrown through the window, who let out a strained sputter as he lay on the ground amidst glass and splintered rock. "These Tharkar came into our territory. *Our* bar!"

"It's Weddin's bar," Riddin said. He fixed the man with a smile whose gaze he hoped instilled just a bit of fear. He kicked the man's boot off the Tharkar on the ground.

"He pays tithe to Khad, don't he?" the dwarf asked, raising his sharp, bearded chin up to meet Riddin's eyes. "Means it's ours, whether the ol' man recognizes that or not."

"Hm." Riddin's fear-filled smile hadn't done the job. He would need to work on that. Instead, Riddin looked to the first man who'd spoken to him: a young dwarf shorter than the rest and twice as wide made of pure muscle without a wisp of hair on him. "Aezik?" Riddin lifted his icing knuckles with a nod.

Aezik's fist collided with the obstinate dwarf's jaw with so much force it could have cracked stone. That being said, it easily cracked bone, and sent a few teeth—along with the dwarf's consciousness—flying from his head. He spun and landed face-first on the broken glass.

Riddin watched as any protesting thought from the other five dwarves vanished.

"Crown-splitter's ass, Aezik," Riddin said. "I asked you to knock some sense into Viz, not hospitalize him."

"Technically," he said. "You didn't ask me to do anythin'. You just said my name. Your princely demeaner's what told me to knock some sense into him. Or, well, outta him, I suppose."

"My 'princely demeaner?'"

"Mhm."

"Right," Riddin couldn't help but chuckle. "And uh, what's my princely demeaner telling you, and the rest of you," Riddin raised his voice for the street to hear, "to do now?"

"Hmm," Aezik said, and he was the only one who spoke. After no one came up with anything, Riddin's smile dropped.

"Go back to the Rock." A shuffle of uncertainty trundled through the crowd. "Now!"

Their apprehension vanished almost as quickly as they did. Riddin blinked, and all five dwarves were at the end of the street, turning the corner upward toward Khad Rock. Aezik was the only one who lagged behind. He picked Viz up, hefted him over his shoulder, and chased after the others, leaving Riddin alone with the Tharkar on the ground.

He hadn't asked Aezik to pick Viz up, though he had wanted him to. Maybe there *was* something to his 'princely demeaner' after all. He hoped so. He would need it for what was next.

Riddin let the ice bag fall to the ground as he squatted next to the Tharkar grunt and reached his hand to his hip to draw his weapon and pull it up between them.

"You're in the wrong part of Mordkin, Tharkar," Riddin said. "Though from the words you were speaking, it sounds like you already knew that much. My question is, why? Why come into Khad territory just to start a fight at my favorite bar?" The grunt's eyes drifted, and Riddin gave him several quick, sharp slaps across his cheek with his free hand. "Hey now, I asked you a question."

"Go fuck yerself!" The grunt's venomous words hit Riddin along with the blood-stained spit.

"Careful now." Riddin pressed the barrel of his weapon beneath the dwarf's jaw, jamming it into the muscle where he knew the pressure would cause it to cramp painfully. "Doesn't seem 'go fuck yerself' was the right answer to my question. Now: why? If I didn't know any better, I'd say you and your friends simply hand a death wish, but the fact they ran for their lives informs me otherwise."

No answer. Riddin pressed the weapon up harder and leaned their knee onto the grunt's chest until their gasp dug the weapon even deeper.

"What were you hoping to accomplish tonight, eh?" Riddin asked. "Did you think we would just roll over? Tharkar hasn't stood a chance against Khad in over two hundred years. What, did little Anez just get tired of watching you drink that piss you serve in your own Krest-damned bar?"

"King Anezendir will break Roan Khad over his knee like the screamin' bitch he is before the night's done! Him, and you, and all the other Khad bastards."

"*King*?" Riddin chuckled. "My, I didn't realize he was in line. Funny, I don't recall stepping down for him." The grunt's jaw clenched in what might have been pain, if it weren't for his eyes flashing wide with fear for just a moment. "Aye, Prince

Riddin Khad, at your service."

"*Prince.*" The grunt spoke with enough distain the word was twisted into a curse on his tongue. Dwarves were good at swearing, but the talent of making any word a swear was a rare skill. Pity.

"Sounds to me like Anez needs a little reminder of Khad's strength." Riddin's finger slid over the weapon's trigger. "You'll do nicely."

Riddin pulled the trigger.

There wasn't even a click.

The Tharkar grunt let out a sputtering chuckle beneath the pressure of Riddin's knee. The chuckle turned into a laugh that echoed through the apprehensive streets with the shame it hammered into Riddin. Rage replaced justice; or perhaps justice was all Riddin thought it was.

He wasn't proud of the noises that escaped his mouth as his boot came down on the Tharkar grunt's head again and again and again. Frustration and anger fueled his unintelligible outbursts like a wounded animal; a mixture of screams and grunts of effort as the grunt's head quickly became mush, then paste, then squelching red mist on the rock-hewn streets. With nothing left to stomp, and the promised silence of the street finally able to return, Riddin regained his composure.

He turned to leave upward—to Khad Rock with the others, or at least toward it—when he saw Weddin staring at the headless body out the broken front window of his bar. He shook.

Trembled, like a flag caught in a strong breeze from the ventilation shafts. Weddin had seen the whole thing.

"Krest-damnit," Riddin said. He took a step toward Weddin, but the man flinched away. Understandable. Instead, Riddin reached into his second coin pouch—he always carried three—and pulled free a gold coin. "Sorry for the mess, Weddin," he said, tossing the coin across the bar's threshold and at the barkeeper's feet. "That's for the trouble. I'll get somebody down to clean all this up by morning, okay?"

The barkeeper didn't speak, and Riddin could understand why. As he turned upward and started his trek up the streets to Khad Rock, Riddin lamented the simple fact that he would need to find another bar to drink at after tonight. At least for the next decade. He would need to give Weddin some rest.

As Riddin made the climb up the slanted streets, he passed by what he could only feel were the failures of his father's leadership. Government soldiers in silver mail armor overlaid with the off-white leather of bat's wings—bleached as close to white as they would ever get—beat down vagrants and enacted justice against petty criminals and homeless with a stern, vengeful hand. Criminals looked to Riddin with some sort of hope; a prayer for relief, while the soldiers looked to him with nodded reverence for the Khad prince, and Riddin couldn't stop for either of them.

The reality was that there wasn't anything for him to do. His power extended only so far, often only to arm's reach. When he was king, perhaps he could do more, but as prince he would waste every second of life settling those minor squabbles between law and crime while more such squabbles would spread throughout Mordkin unimpeded. As king, he would enact real change. Lasting change.

He wouldn't rid Mordkin of petty crime altogether—that was the foolish dream of the government's law. Nor would he rid the city of the law—that was the foolish dream of the unorganized. The answer didn't lie in riddance. It lied in safety. After all, for organized crime to flourish, it needed to be safe from the powers of law as well as the filth of unorganized crime.

And every city needed organized crime to flourish.

After an hour of weaving through streets and heading upward, Riddin saw the grand, towering structure of Khad Rock at the top of Mordkin's slant. The highest point in the city, and the tallest building in a city of tiered structures, his home stood as a castling testament to the power that rested inside.

At the foot of the stairs leading up to the door, Riddin cut left; twisting through a side door and into Orin's workshop. The spindly man—and he *was* a man—sat on a low chair with his knees high and spread to either side, his body stooping over a table built, like everything in Mordkin, for dwarves. His boney elbows rested on the table and supported the weight of his curved back as he poked and prodded his favorite pastime invention with tweezers; something he called a wrist watch.

Riddin pulled the weapon from its sheathe and tossed it onto the table with the jolting clatter of heavy metal on hard wood. Orin jumped, breaking free from his mediation only to scurry to the weapon and pick it up.

"Careful!" Orin said. "This is a delicate instrument with the destructive power of—"

"It still doesn't work," Riddin said. "Tried using it to teach a lesson. Didn't even fire once." Riddin looked to the table at the previous prototype displayed on two raised metal prongs. "At least the last one could *do* something."

"What do you mean 'it doesn't work?' Was it a misfire? Click-no-bang? How many times did you pull the trigger?"

"Twice. And no, not a misfire. No-click, no-bang."

"Hmm, sounds like a malfunction in the trigger mechanism. Perhaps something become dislodged."

Orin brought the weapon beneath a large magnifying glass attached to a spring arm and started examining it. Riddin watched from over the man's hunched shoulder as he removed the hilt plate and exposed the inner mechanism. Except...

"Look. The spin wheel," Riddin said. "There's too much space without the manual actuator. The trigger doesn't even activate it now."

"I see." Orin chewed his bottom lip thoughtfully, pushing the skin of his lips between his teeth with his fingers to bit it off. He must have overchewed his nails again. "I could...fill the empty space with flux. Not a pretty solution, but it would fix the problem. Hopefully."

Riddin considered this. If it worked, the inner mechanics

would be ugly, but it would be a functioning prototype, but it wouldn't be a proper weapon. Like a chipped dagger. It would still cut, but it wasn't prefered.

"No," Riddin said. "Cut a new frame. Refit the pieces to reduce wasted space. I'll take the other one for now." Riddin grabbed the other prototype off the table and fit it back into his hand. Orin gave him a warning look, but he had learned long ago not to keep Riddin from what he wanted by force.

"I haven't made any changes beyond the repair," Orin said. "It still suffers from the same catastrophic failure."

"That's fine. At least I'll have one shot. What matters is I'll have a weapon."

"Are you expecting to need one soon?"

The question was genuine; the only kind of question Orin knew how to ask. Riddin, in turn, only gave the man genuine answers.

"Maybe," he said. "I'll know more once I speak to my father. For now," he tapped a thick finger on the dismantled prototype beneath Orin's gaze, "work on this. Quickly, but carefully. I'll need my own Throat-Cleaver soon."

Orin scoffed. "Throat-Cleaver. If you had designed a Throat-Cleaver you wouldn't have needed my fingers. This isn't some simpleton's sword. This? This is a work of art."

"Right now it's trash. It's your job to make it art. So get painting."

"*Painting.*" The artificer rolled his eyes, but got to work without complaint.

Riddin slid the faulty weapon into its sheathe at his hip and used the connecting doors, steep stairs, and straight corridors to arrive at his father's throne.

Where the entire Rock was grand and imposing, the throne room itself was small. Intimate. Being King of Mordkin's underground wasn't a position of rule and presence fit for large, echoing chambers supported by rows of huge columns made of marble. It was dirty work, conducted in the light but planned in the shadows, and King Roan Khad's throne was where all the shadows met. There were no barren walls because they were set with doors that spread throughout the Rock like arteries from a heart. The throne was simple; cut from the same rock it was still connected to. The same rock that cut five shallow steps down to the floor where those who came to seek the King's orders would kneel.

Where Captain Henka knelt now, her pregnant belly struggling to contain her unborn child beneath her silver and off-white uniform.

"Riots have begun in the streets," Henka said. Her voice came from deep within her chest and filled the small room; meeting everyone's ears. Looking around, Riddin recognized Aezik in attendance, on the side of the room that denoted he had already spoken to the King. Aezik met Riddin's eyes and nodded. Great.

"Riots are the law's problem," the King said. "You trouble

me with your own failings, Captain?"

"We're keeping the peace, King Roan."

"Then why the fuck are you kneeling at *my* throne and telling me about *riots*?"

"Because they involve your men," Henka said, looking up at Riddin's father. "The Tharkar are starting riots throughout Mordkin, targeting Khad-owned streets, and *your men* are making matters worse."

"They're defending our kingdom."

"They're destroying it, along with killing the Tharkar. If you don't de-escalate the situation soon, things will only get worse."

King Roan stood, using his wide two-handed sword as a staff with the blade dug into the stone. "Tharkar begin riots, Khad defend themselves, and it is somehow *my* responsibility to de-escalate? Do you know that Anezendir calls himself King now? He threatens my rule, and you ask me to, what, be a good bitch, roll over, and take it?"

"I expect you to be King."

"You expect me to be the law!" Roan lifted his great sword into the air, the gem in its hilt twinkling with an inner light that sent blue lightning arcing along the blade's path. "I earned my place on this throne with blood, Captain! Innocent or guilty, it didn't matter: Throat-Cleaver silenced them all. I rid Mordkin's government of my competition so they could rule the city, and I could rule its crime, and now that someone threatens my reign—after two-hundred years—you ask me to concede? Concede the peace of your city's underground?"

King Roan took the five shallow steps down to Henka, Throat-Cleaver drawn. Riddin tensed, his hand finding the grip of his weapon as his father came close.

Henka's gaze never fell from the king's eyes.

"Peace in Mordkin is threatened, Captain," Roan said. "Your soldiers need you. Go. Do what must be done, and *trust* that I will do likewise." Roan leaned forward, blue lightning glinting in his furious eyes the same as the gem of his sword. "But remember, *Captain*: there is only one name that matters in Mordkin. Do you know what name that is?"

Henka's gaze faltered for a moment, her face twisting in a moment of pain Riddin couldn't find the source of. It was enough to make a wicked grin spread over his father's face.

"Khad," Henka said.

"Khad." Roan nodded. He stood and turned his back on Henka, taking the shallow stairs one at a time back up to his throne, Throat-Cleaver his sword and cane. "You'll do well to remember that in the future."

Henka looked at Riddin, her expression surprise and worry, before she stood and walked to the far side of the room; joining Aezik instead of leaving.

Curious.

"Riddin!" Roan called from his throne. "Where have you been, my boy?"

"Gathering information," he said, simply. He took Henka's place as he knelt before the throne's steps. "Though it seems you're already aware of all I've learned. Anez Tharkar calls himself King, and his men are causing trouble in the streets."

"Yes, yes. The bastard thinks he can steal my throne. Steal *your* throne. But by your tone, it does not fill you with the same rage it does me."

"The man's a fool, father. He thinks riots will win him a throne, and sends ants to poke at spiders."

A sneer winced onto King Roan's lips. "Always so *poetic*. What will you do about Anezendir's treason, then?"

"Father?"

Roan lifted Throat-Cleaver from the ground and rested the broad sword on his lap. He ran his hand across the blade as though petting an animal, and lightning arced between the metal and his palm.

"I will spare you the history lesson I just gave the Captain," Roan said. "Anezendir threatens your future throne. It is time you take your own blade to his throat and earn my throne."

"What? Father, that's madness."

"Madness?" Roan's eyes glinted with the dangers of just that.

"Mordkin is a powder keg, ready to ignite with a stray spark. Killing Anezendir would set the entire city ablaze with war. Not just between Tharkar and Khad, but everyone: Durza, Prazed, the countless Unnamed, everyone."

"War is a king-maker, Riddin! It either drives away cowards or kills them. The strong rise to the surface, and society is made stronger for it."

"But shouldn't we *try* to maintain peace?" Riddin asked, his gaze glancing to Henka. "There is no organized crime if there is no law to work beneath."

King Roan sucked his teeth as his lips curled up in snarled anger. "I see. So, then, I have raised a coward."

"What?"

"A coward!" Roan's voice filled the small room, fanning the flames of embarrassment that crept up Riddin's neck. "Rather than make yourself worthy of a throne, you would give it to a lesser dwarf for the sake of peace and ease? You would let the city you could lead to greatness wither and die to *weakness*?"

"No!"

"Then prove it! Bring me that Tharkar bastard's broken crown, along with his head, and I will *give* you my throne."

Those in attendance murmured while Riddin's teeth clenched. He studied the ground; the fractured lines that threatened the faults of the rock the throne was hewn from. Faults that would crumble if they were pressed.

"I will go." Riddin said. He stood, turned, and walked out of the throne room, the crowd's murmurs, the crackling of blue lightning arcing from his father's blade, and a pair of hurried footfalls following him out.

"Where are you going?" Henka's voice called from behind.

"To pay Anez Tharkar a visit," he said.

"You can't! You said it yourself, the city is a powder keg. If you kill Anezendir, the whole city will burst into flame, and just because we're carved from stone doesn't mean we don't burn."

"I know that!" Riddin turned to look Henka in the eyes. Her hard face soft with worry as she held her stomach with one hand and a sword in the other. Riddin walked up to her, placing his own hand on her stomach as he gazed into her eyes, close enough to smell the intoxicating, earthen scent of her breath.

"I'm not going to kill Anezendir," Riddin said. "I still think peace is an option, no matter what my father says."

"But...but he's demanded his head."

"And he demanded death to unhand my mother. Just because he demands something doesn't mean it must be so."

"You're not death," Henka said. She leaned into him and he kissed her forehead.

"Not if I don't have to be."

Riddin pulled Henka close, wrapping his arms around her as he turned to look at the other person whose footsteps had accompanied him out of the throne room. He shared a look with Aezik, and the young brute nodded his thick head knowingly.

"Of course I'll come with you, Riddin."

"Thank you."

As Riddin pulled away from Henka, he grabbed the short sword from her hand and drew it into his own. "Stay safe while I'm away." He placed his free hand on her stomach once again.

"Both of you."

He turned from her before her gaze could change his mind and walked with Aezik down the corridor and out into the city.

The mood of the encroaching night was thick with apprehension that wrapped around Riddin the moment he stepped foot outside the Rock. It was partly to do with his task; meet with Anezendir Tharkar, the man who wanted to kill his father, and probably Riddin himself, and convince him instead of peace. The other part was much more external.

Riddin, like many dwarves, had been born and raised in Mordkin; the city much less developed those sixty-odd years ago. While there hadn't been a city-wide conflict like the war that had put his father in power over the underground in that time, there were many moments of tension. Whenever they built, the city itself coiled; tensing like a sharp breath before known pain. Like Throat-Cleaver's gem, Riddin was convinced there was some sort of magic involved. An actual, physical manifestation of the city's collective psychology, buried somewhere deep inside the earth.

Of course, Riddin had a wild imagination.

The trek downward toward Tharkar Rock took Riddin and Aezik past a city that slowly devolved into crumbling homes and outright violence. A part of the city deemed lawless, thanks to the soldier's abandonment of it. Aezik hefted his warhammer in response to the lingering stares and crouching shadows, and Riddin's grip tightened on Henka's sword while his other hand rested to the hilt of the prototype weapon at his hip.

As they moved past, the not-so-hidden Tharkar moved around them; washing up behind them like great eddies in a pool and cutting off their means of quick escape. Riddin didn't have any intention of turning around before meeting with Anezendir, but knowing he couldn't was another reality entirely. Still, no ambush came as they finally arrived at the threshold of Tharkar Rock.

Where Khad Rock was great and towering, Tharkar Rock was diminished: nearly indistinguishable from the other buildings that surrounded it. When Riddin stepped inside he was greeted with a bastardization of the throne room he had just been in.

It was small. Not for reason or by design, but by necessity. It connected to various doors haphazardly, lacking the organization of Khad Rock as they branched to the neighboring homes that had been grafted onto this one. The ground was uneven; splintered and cracked by long shifting faults and sending sheets of rock up like tiny mountains.

The room was crowded. Standing room only, including where the throne would have been, if it had been more than a crumbling mess. And there, standing at the end, lit dramatically by the ghostly green gas lamp sconces was Anezendir Tharkar. Dark, with even darker hair that covered his head and face like a mane. Only his eyes, red as the dyed clothes he wore, shone through; piercing Riddin with a rage and fury no words could ever communicate. He stood hunched with the burden of leading the poorest named family in Mordkin for the last hundred and twenty years.

"I do not even need to summon the pup," Anezendir said. "He comes crawling to me, though I am curious if it is in surrender or sacrifice."

Aezik's gloves creaked as his grip tightened on his war hammer.

"Neither," Riddin said. "I come to speak peace, Anez."

"Only after kicking my man's head in. Tell me, Riddin Khad, what makes you believe I would want peace? Have the battles my men have started not communicated my intentions?"

"Battles?" Riddin asked. "You...mean the riots? The ones we and the city soldiers have snuffed out easily enough? A bit self-aggrandizing to call them 'battles,' Anez."

"My name is Anezendir, boy."

"I apologize, Anezendir." Riddin looked around the room at the tensing profiles of the Tharkar. He counted twenty, but he knew there were more in the shadows. There were always more. "Tell me, do you think you can win a war with Khad? Against King Roan? Wouldn't peace be preferable?"

"Preferable, aye. And we will have peace, once Roan Khad is dead, and I sit on the throne."

"When my father dies, I will be the one to inherit his throne."

Anezendir barked a laugh that rippled through the attendees to their audience. Riddin glanced around, searching for an exit. He really hadn't thought this through.

"The only way to obtain power is through war," Anezendir said. "Your father understood that two-hundred years ago. Dwarves have understood it much longer than that." Anezendir stepped closer to Riddin, hatred spewing from his red eyes. As he drew near, Riddin could see the man's teeth had been filed and sharpened to points. "Power can only be taken, pup. 'Inheritance' is for men. 'Giving' is for elves. Taking. That is the way of dwarves."

"It doesn't have to be," Riddin said. "We can find a new way. Here, now, together."

"Reach a decision that results in a system that only benefits you? I think not."

Riddin heard the swooshing through the air a moment before Aezik threw him down onto the ground. The sword swung by one of the Tharkar flew through the air where his neck had been.

Aezik swung his war hammer in response. It battered aside three swords attempting to block its momentum, knocking one Tharkar's head in and sending the others flying across the room. More filled their places, stabbing at Aezik with swords and daggers that he broke or brushed away with the handle of his hammer. He was too busy with those in front of him, however, to notice the Tharkar raising a hammer of his own from behind, ready to swing it down onto Aezik's head.

Riddin drew the weapon from his hip, aimed, and fired in one fluid motion. The trigger clicked, activating the spinwheel inside and sending a bullet of condensed electricity shooting from the barrel and straight through the Tharkar's head, and it didn't stop there. The condensed electricity ricocheted off the stone ceiling and came down into the back of another grunt; dropping his guard as Aezik's war hammer found his head.

If the Tharkar were surprised by the prototype, they spent no time recovering. One of the grunts kicked the weapon from Riddin's hand and pinned his wrist to the ground. Riddin thrust up awkwardly with Henka's sword in his off hand, stabbing the grunt between the legs and into his torso. He collapsed to his knees—and onto Riddin—in his pain, and Riddin had to spend a considerable amount of effort getting the man's body off him as he stood up.

Aezik was a man possessed; his war hammer squelching flesh and crumpling armor as its swings were powered by his immense strength. With Riddin finally back on his feet, he could finally help, and his sword found purchase in a number of Tharkar before the fighting froze all at once.

Anezendir stood pointing the barrel of Riddin's weapon right at him, his red eyes showing the smile his black beard hid.

"You fight well, Riddin Khad," Anezendir said. "But I won't let you take my power."

Riddin watched as the false king's finger squeezed against the trigger. "Anez, don't!" He flinched away, behind a Tharkar grunt, as Anez pulled the trigger.

This prototype was nearly perfect. It had followed

Riddin's designs exactly, but there had been a fatal flaw in that design neither Riddin nor Orin could have found before it was built. Luckily, when Riddin had tested it the first time, the recoil of the gun had snapped it from his hands. The second shot had happened when it hit the ground behind him. The result was that Riddin was alive, and that Orin, who had been standing nearby, now had lightning shaped scars running from his calf to the opposite shoulder blade.

This time, the second shot was in Anezendir Tharkar's hand.

Lightning exploded from the weapon's hilt; its spinwheel over-correcting the energy requirements and super charging the shot. the metal frame stood little chance as the energy shattered it; sending shards throughout the room and into the back of the Tharkar grunt Riddin had taken cover behind. Somewhere behind him, Riddin heard Aezik cry out in pain, and his war hammer thumped onto the ground soon after.

The exploding weapon had taken Anezendir's arm; his body scorched with electric burns and the clothing on his right side fuzed to his body. His beard and hair were singed off just enough for Riddin to see the horror on his face right before the screaming started.

The throne room erupted in panic, Anezendir's screams adding to those of pain and horror from the other grunts in attendance as they ran into one another, bumping and trampling as those that could fled through the various doors.

No one went to help their king, even as his screams faded along with his life.

Pain lanced Riddin's side. One of the metal shards of the prototype had found its way to him after all. He struggled to look around; the Tharkar grunt he had hidden behind dead and fallen on top of him. Another dead man pinning him to the ground.

Until suddenly, he wasn't. The monstrous form of Aezik pushed the man off Riddin as he dragged himself over on his own injured leg.

"Not the greatest weapon," Aezik grunted. "If it kills the person holding the damn thing." He pushed himself into a kneeling position and helped Riddin onto his feet. "You need to get out of here."

Riddin was about to agree wholeheartedly, but couldn't find the words. His head swam as he struggled to keep it upright. Something came out of his mouth, but not even he could tell what it was.

"Riddin? Riddin!"

Aezik hefted him up into his arms as the sound of encroaching footfalls came to answer the screams of their dying king, and that was the last thing Riddin remembered.

* * *

RIDDIN WAS NO stranger to pain. Well, physical pain. He had been stabbed, trampled, kicked, cut, bludgeoned; there was a lot of pain that could be experienced in sixty-three years, especially for the son of Roan Khad.

The difference between that pain, and the pain that shocked him awake as Orin slid the slivers of metal out of his writhing body, was that there was no adrenaline coursing through him. It had been spent, and the pain of the needles pincushioning him had become something familiar in his unconscious. Not pleasant, but tolerable. Now they ripped like scratching ice; leaving his skin burnt and raw while making him feel cold as more blood left through the holes.

"Hold him down," Orin said, and strong arms—Aezik's arms—came down to do just that.

"Aaaaaa-I'll fucking kill you!" Riddin's screams of torment turned into a roar of fury.

"You don't mean that," Aezik said. There was that same look in his eyes as he stared down at Riddin, looming over him with his paralyzing weight, that he'd had in front of Weddin's Bar. The look of knowing without being told.

Orin ran stitches all over Riddin's body, which were thankfully less painful. Riddin was able to slow his breathing and calm his heart: which came with the challenge of staving off another bout of unconsciousness. While Orin worked, for the first time, Riddin could hear more screams coming from outside the artificer's workshop. Screams, clangs of steel, and the explosions of black powder.

"What the fuck did I miss?" Riddin asked. "How long was

I out?"

"Not long," Aezik answered. "An hour, maybe two at most. I had to set you down a few times to kill some Tharkar, otherwise it would've been sooner. I tried to be gentle."

"You were a great deal gentler than Orin!" he said between gasps of pain. Orin simply continued his thankless work. "What's going on outside?"

"War," Aezik said, simply. "Mordkin's been threatening to boil, you saw it yourself. You *said it* yourself. Now Anezendir's dead, and the Tharkar're blaming you and your father."

"It's been two...hours!"

"Only took thirty seconds."

Riddin took stock of what Aezik was saying. Everything he had been trying to prevent by going to Anezendir was now tearing his city apart. Skirmishes would be happening all over Mordkin, catching innocent civilians in the crossfire between Tharkar and Khad. Between...

"There aren't enough Tharkar to start a war," Riddin said. Orin had finished stitching and had moved on to wrapping him in bandages. "Who's leading them? With Anezendir gone."

Aezik gave a shrug. "Durza? Prazed? Take your pick."

"They're united against us? Against Khad Rock?"

"United's a...strong word. Temporarily aligned's more like. Still, you're right about the numbers. Even if all the families were organized and unified, Khad'd still outnumber them two to one. More, after what you and I did to the Anez and his Tharkar."

"So it's only a matter of time before this is all over," Riddin said. With Orin's help, he stood from the table. "And my father will still be the one on the throne."

"Prince Riddin..." Aezik looked nervous for the first time. "Just before I came into the shop here—"

"You mean broke down my door," Orin said, matter-of-factly.

"—Khad Rock...it was burning."

Shock and confusion caused the blood to leave Riddin's head, and Aezik rushed forward to keep him upright; helping a faulting Orin. Khad Rock burned, the home his father had built over the last two centuries, was burning? The seat of underground power in Mordkin was threatened?

Then an even more sickening thought found purchase in his mind and sent fear into his heart.

"Henka," Riddin said. "Is she still in the Rock?"

"I don't know," Aezik said. "I haven't been there. Like I said, it—"

Riddin pushed away from Aezik and Orin, supporting himself against the table he had just been laying on. He looked around. This was Orin's shop, wasn't it? It took him only a moment to find what he was searching for.

"This'll work?" Riddin asked Orin. He held the prototype up. "You've machined a new casing? Reordered the insides, like we talked about?"

"It...hasn't been tested," Orin said.

"It's about to be." Riddin slid the weapon into his hip sheathe and walked past Orin toward the door. It *had* been broken in. Then hastily barricaded against the war waging outside.

Riddin looked back at Aezik. The thick dwarf didn't need to be asked as he grabbed his gore-covered war hammer from where it rested against the wall and moved the barricades aside.

"Riddin..." Orin's voice trailed off, and Riddin turned to look at the aging man; younger than he was, but older in race. "Be careful."

Riddin nodded, and together with Aezik, they pushed out into the city.

Mordkin had been built from the remnants of an old mine. Slowly the mine had given away to buildings, with Dwarves choosing to live as well as work there. It had been built with ventilation in mind, and as the city grew deeper and deeper into the mountain, uncovering deposits of natural gas that then became street lamps, and fresh water wells that then became the city's reservoir, those vents had been maintained and expanded. They brought fresh air in from the outside to replace the stale air that they snatched away. There was, on a good day, a slight breeze that would sweep through the city, whistling as it draped itself around the cut stone.

Now, as the streets of Mordkin burned, those same breezes showed the churning eddies of black smoke above Riddin's head. There were no stars under the mountain, but the smoke made it impossible to see anything about the city's third level. No amount of ventilation, no matter how well planned and how well produced, could keep up with burning stone and roiling flames.

A Tharkar grunt dove out of the smoke, landing a dozen feet in front of Riddin and charging without a moment's hesitation. With a speed that made Riddin's fresh stitches ache and tear, he drew his weapon and pulled the trigger.

Condensed blue lightning shot out of the cylinder and through the dwarf's chest. When he didn't slow, Riddin chanced another pull of the trigger, and was rewarded with another clean shot—straight through the charging dwarf's head. The Tharkar's feet quit moving as his body sailed forward and slammed face-first onto the hewn street. Eyes wide and lifeless.

"Glad this one works," Aezik grunted next to him.

Riddin nodded. "Come on," he said. "We need to get to the Rock."

Riddin wished he could say that was the only man he killed on his way upward to Khad Rock. To Henka. But he couldn't. Aezik handled most of the killing; protecting him from Tharkar and Durza as they stumbled out of the choking smoke to find them. He never saw Prazed colors, though. There was that, at least.

By the time they reached Khad Rock, flames burst from the grand entryway and windows as though burning with holy fire, and Riddin had killed seventeen dwarves: all trying to kill him first.

Riddin and Aezik secreted away through the passage he

had used earlier that day. Krest below, had it really been only a few hours ago? Together they wound through the corridors and burning chambers of the Rock until they heard a woman's screams. Henka's screams.

Riddin rushed after them, but quickly found the passageway blocked, the soot-stained rock crumbled.

"Double back!" Riddin said, choking in the smoke. "To the throne room. We'll use one of the other passages!"

If a protest had come to Aezik's lips, he didn't have time to utter it before Riddin squeezed past the thick dwarf and rushed on stumbling footsteps down the corridors and into the throne room.

Throat-Cleaver crackled with blue lightning as it sailed through the necks of three Tharkar dwarves at once. King Roan stood in front of his throne, smiling wider than Riddin had ever seen before as he welcomed the assailants through the corridor that led to the front gate: the large Tharkar force cut down to a steady, single file flow from the narrow corridors. Still, they filled the room quickly. Dozens of Tharkar stood ready to charge Riddin's father for the taste of glory that came with killing a King.

Then they spotted Riddin.

Aezik beat down the Tharkar assailants while Riddin drew his weapon and fired into the crowd. Behind him, King Roan laughed with awe and joy while Riddin's stomach twisted as seventeen deaths became eighteen, nineteen, twenty, twenty-one.

A Tharkar pushed through Aezik's swinging hammer and tackled Riddin to the ground. His body wailing in agony—knowing all of Orin's hard work stitching him closed had been for nothing—Riddin pulled his weapon up to the Tharkar's head and pulled the trigger. Twenty-one became twenty-two as gore exploded from the back of the dwarf's skull along with the bolt of blue lightning.

When Riddin pushed the body off of himself, it was a struggle to stand. He crawled away from the fighting until his back touched a wall he could use to press against and stand up. He fired shot after shot into the crowd, unable to help Aezik or his father push the front as his bloody total continued to climb.

That's when Henka's screams came echoing through the corridors once more. He pushed himself off the wall, but quickly found himself back against it, only able to aim the weapon and pull the trigger. He could barely move. Desperately he searched the throne room for something he could do. *Anything* he could do.

He found Aezik's eyes.

For all Aezik's talk of 'princely demeanor,' Riddin would not have believed it if it weren't for that one, singular moment. The moment where their eyes met: Aezik's hammer crushing the skull of a Durza while Riddin fired indiscriminately into the growing pile of bodies, and Aezik didn't need to hear Riddin ask. He didn't even hesitate. Following the momentum of his war hammer, Aezik launched himself sideways and away, through one of the doors to the throne room's right and after the screams of the woman Riddin loved.

Between the pain that riddled him, the screams of those he killed, and the bloodthirsty laughter from his father, Riddin didn't know how long he spent fighting those that flooded into the throne room. He didn't know what became of Henka; her screams slowly fading away in the heat of war. He didn't know what became of Aezik.

What he did know, was by the time the Tharkar and Durza stopped swarming into the throne room, and the fires that burned the castle had begun to die out from lack of fuel and the smothering of Khad soldiers that still lived, Riddin had killed one-hundred and forty-two dwarves with the weapon he had hoped would never kill anyone.

"My son!" Roan bellowed. Blue lightning crackled from his eyes the same as from the gem in Throat-Cleaver's hilt. "All this time, I was afraid you would never take a life, and yet here you are, taking them with the soulless range of a weapon *you* designed!"

King Roan took the five shallow steps up to his throne and slumped into his seat. The sounds of fighting from outside now died down as well, the war, as Aezik had said, was quick. The Tharkar didn't have the numbers. Their only hope had been their assault on Khad Rock.

Whisperer Kren slithered his way out of one of the doors behind the throne and came up to his father's side.

"The war is won, my king," Kren said. "You have shown those who would take your throne that you are no less fierce than you were—"

"The war is not won, Kren," Roan said. Despite Riddin's pain, he looked into his father's eyes, crackling with a rage-filled madness. "Where were the city soldiers? We did not need their aid, yet still, they did not come."

"Hmmm, yes. Quite right, my king. The city's soldiers were cowards to the end. They waited to hear whose voice would ring triumphant in the night. Only then did they choose to support."

"The city guard are meant to protect the city," Riddin said, earning his father's cold stare. "They are not your soldiers."

"They should be!" Roan said. "It's time they came to heel. Time they learned their place, like the Tharkar and the Durza and the fucking Prazed." Roan leaned forward in his throne, staring wide-eyed at Riddin. "With that weapon in your hand, and Throat-Cleaver in mine, we could take this city. *Really* take it. No more hiding in the shadows, ruling the Krest-damn underground. I could become the law. Fuck, Riddin, after what we've done today, you and I *alone* could take down the council: Krest's name as my own!"

Riddin stared up at his father. He held his side—out of habit and comfort more than actual aid. In his other hand, he held his weapon; shaking in his grip as his fingers remembered the vibrating recoil of one-hundred and forty-two deaths.

Somewhere in Khad Rock, Henka had stopped screaming. Was she dead, too? Had Aezik been too late? What about him? Was Aezik counted among the fallen? Was his death on Riddin's conscience, too?

"No..." The words escaped Riddin's lips in a breath.

"What did you say, boy?" Roan asked. "Come on, speak up! We cannot make you a king if you can't speak properly!"

"I said no."

As though in a trance, Riddin raised his hand and aimed the weapon at his father. With a pull of a trigger that surprised himself and the king in equal measure, one-hundred forty-two became one-hundred forty-three as the bolt of condensed lightning shot out to meet his father square between the eyes.

Roan Khad slumped forward in his throne. Throat-Cleaver twisted unnaturally in his limp grasp, unable to support his weight as he fell onto the steps. Blood pooled around his head like a halo, the back of his skull blown open in a mess of gore that matched the splatter on the throne's high back.

The throne room grew silent. Those few in attendance refused to speak as fear blanketed over them. Riddin stepped over his father's body and collapsed onto the throne. His father had been right. Anezendir 'Tharkar had been right. Power, even if Riddin wanted to use that power to restore peace and ease tension, had to be taken. That was what it meant to be a dwarf.

"M-my king, I—"

Whisperer Kren would never get the chance to whisper hatred and distrust in Riddin's ear, because Riddin wouldn't give him that chance. His sentence cut off at the pull of the trigger as the dwarf became the one hundred fortieth death at Riddin's hands. Or was he one hundred forty-one?

"Go out into the city," Riddin said. His voice was low, but carried over the swelling Khad grunts who had once questioned his strength. "If any Tharkar or Durza still fight, kill them. If they flee, let them. I will deal with the families when we put out the fires of war and the smoke of Mordkin clears enough for me to see the crystal stars. Go! Heal the city."

And they did. They funneled out of the throne room, some carrying the bodies of those Riddin and his father had slain, though no one touched Roan. No one came close.

Until, that is, Aezik squeezed through a doorway to the right. He paused only for a moment as he stared at Riddin on the throne and the dead King at his feet. Long enough for Riddin to notice the bundle of cloth he held in his arms before the thick dwarf took the five approaching steps. He stepped wide over the fault that ran up the steps, and Riddin noticed for the first time that it had grown in the chaos. The fissure was worse. He would have to repair that at some point.

"My King," Aezik said. "Henka sleeps, but she is well." He pushed the bundle of cloth into Riddin's arm, and the light weight of its contents pressed heavy against his heart. "She has named him Rime, my King."

Riddin looked down at his son. He had been mostly cleaned, but not washed, and the blood of birth was still evident in the crevices of his closed eyes and his light hair. The smell of iron mixed with stone as it touched Riddin's nose.

When Riddin looked up at his own father, Throat-Cleaver's blue gem still crackled in its hilt on the ground. The power of it called to him, as it always had.

Riddin raised his weapon and shattered the magical gem with a pull of the trigger.

He looked back down at his son. He looked like neither Riddin nor Henka. Perhaps that would come with age, or perhaps, like Riddin, Rime was destined to stand apart from his family.

He looked into his other hand at the weapon that had brought the Tharkar to heel. The weapon that had killed his father and the whisperer in his ear. The weapon that he had designed, that Orin had crafted, and that had placed him on the throne of Khad Rock when the promise of his blood had failed.

It wasn't just a weapon.

It was a King-Maker.

About the Author

QUAIN HOLTEY has been writing since before he could read. He would often beg his family, friends, pre-school teachers, and everyone else who would listen to read about his magical worlds and daring characters when they were little more than illegible scribbles in the rough shape of paragraphs and pages. Later, he learned to read and form mostly coherent sentences.

Not much else has changed.